D1497827

A Woman of No Character

A WOMAN OF NO CHARACTER

An Autobiography of Mrs Manley

FIDELIS MORGAN

faber and faber
LONDON · BOSTON

First published in 1986 by
Faber and Faber Limited
3 Queen Square London WC1N 3AU

Photoset and printed in Great Britain by
Redwood Burn Limited
Trowbridge Wiltshire
All rights reserved

© Fidelis Morgan 1986

British Library Cataloguing in Publication Data

Morgan, Fidelis
A woman of no character.
1. Manley Mrs—Biography 2. Authors, English
—17th century—Biography 3. Authors, English
—18th century—Biography
I. Title
823'.5   PR3545.M8Z/
ISBN 0–571–13934–5

To cousin Lynda
A Phoebe Crackenthorpe of our times

'Mrs Manley, a woman of no character.'

G. M. Trevelyan, *England Under Queen Anne*
Volume III, Peace and the Protestant Succession
London 1930–34, p. 38

Acknowledgements

I would like to thank

Major E. C. Weaver MBE, honorary archivist, Grenadier Guards; Dr Eveline Cruickshanks, History of Parliament Trust; Jackie Johnson, Sandra Winchester and Paul O'Hanlon at Battersea Reference Library; Marion Roberts of Wrexham Maelor Library; G. T. Knight of Redruth Library; The British Library; Westminster Reference Library; The Bodleian Library; Liverpool University Library; Balham lending library; Dale Spender; The Fawcett Library; The Guildhall; the chief archivist, Windsor Castle; The Société Jerséiaise; Suffolk County Library; The Revd Pryse-Hawkins, St Benet's, Paul's Wharf; Jocelyn, Jane Shilling and Patricia Robertson, Paddy, Pam, Lynda and Celia.

Contents

A Note on the Text

In selecting the writing of Mrs Manley for this book I have used all the episodes included within her published writings which are widely acknowledged to be autobiographical. I have also included, in order to fill out the areas of her life which she did not cover in her fictions, some of her private letters, extracts from her plays, etc., which were published within, or soon after, her lifetime.

I have arranged these autobiographical snippets in their true chronological order, as far as we know it.

In The Adventures of Rivella *her story is told in the third person by 'Sir Charles Lovemore'; elsewhere it is usually told in the first person, Mrs Manley in various disguises.*

In order to assist the narrative thrust I have bridged the gaps with short links explaining who is talking to whom and where.

Where Mrs Manley has not described events which are important to the understanding of her life as a whole, I have written chapters which include as many Manley quotes as possible.

I have cut interjections which interrupt the continuous line of the story.

Except in the Prologue and Epilogue (and in chapter 9, A Bristol Intrigue, where identification is practically impossible) I have replaced the romantic names with the generally accepted identifications of the actual people in Mrs Manley's life. A key in reverse to all names used is included in the Appendix.

I have modernized spelling and punctuation throughout.

In order to make the distinction clear, passages directly quoted from Mrs Manley are set in roman *type, and my own commentary in italic.*

The texts used are as follows:

The Adventures of Rivella, *1714. (No publisher on title page. E. Curll)*
Court Intrigues . . ., *1711. (John Morphew & James Woodward)*
Letters Written by Mrs Manley, *1696. (R.B.)*
The Lost Lover, *1696. (R. Bentley, F. Saunders, J. Knapton, R. Willington)*
The Royal Mistress, *1696. (R. Bentley, F. Saunders & J. Knapton)*
Secret Memoirs . . . from the New Atalantis, *1709. (J. Morphew & J. Woodward)*

A NOTE ON MRS MANLEY'S CHRISTIAN NAME

In 1893, in an article entitled 'Mary de la Riviere Manley', that solid reference work The Dictionary of National Biography *started a trail of red herrings in the search for the Christian name and date of birth of the celebrated author of the* Atalantis, *Mrs Manley.*

Eleven years later the list of errata to the DNB *compounds this mistake, citing Sloane ms. 1708, f. 117. On inspection, Sloane 1708,* Nativities *by F. Barnard, seems to be a birthday book frugally scattered with dates of birth of the famous (the Queen of Bohemia), the unknown (Richard Bill, scrivener), the notorious (an Italian that could, or pretended, change ♀ in ☉), and, on f. 117, 'Mary Manly Ap 7:63 H 3:30pm ♀ Londini'. There is no qualifying description, nothing which identifies this Ms Manly with the Mrs Manley popularly known as Atalantic Dela.*

Mrs Manley always called herself Delarivier or an abbreviation of this. In the excellent American scholarship on the life and work of Mrs Manley it has been decided that she should be called Delariviere. (See Patricia Koster's brilliant sleuthing in 'Delariviere Manley and the DNB', Eighteenth Century Life 3, 1977 pp. 106–11.)

I accept that Mary should be dropped immediately. However, Mrs Manley consistently spelled her name DELARIVIER, *and her name is no more an exercise in French grammar than mine is one in Latin. I am frequently annoyed by people who 'correct' my Christian name to Fidelia to suit their notion of accuracy. However usual or correct the spelling Delariviere may be, I believe that if the lady spelled it without the final 'e', the least we can do is join her.*

Records of Mrs Manley's Christian name in its various forms are:

1691   Dela *(Baptism record of her son)*
1696   Delarivier *(Dedication to* Letters, *Dedication to* The Royal Mischief)
        Dela *(Letter 1,* Letters, *Poem to Agnes de Castro)*
1717   De la Rivier *(Dedication to* Lucius)
1720   De la Rivier *(Dedication to* Lucius)
1720   Dela (The Power of Love)
1724   Delarivier *(her will, twice, and the inscription of her tombstone)*
All other known letters in her own hand are signed D. Manley.

The two biographical dictionaries published during her lifetime also use the name Delarivier:

1699   Langbaine, Lives and Characters *(twice Delarivier)*
1719   Giles Jacob, The Poetical Register *(De la Rivier)*

Although modern practice in addressing women is a hotchpotch of Miss, Mrs and the rather clumsy Ms, I have kept to the seventeenth- and eighteenth-century use of Mrs. Mrs was short for mistress, and any adult woman, married or single, was addressed thus (unless of course she was a Duchess or had some similar title). Miss was saved for children and tarts, and was a mild term of abuse when applied to adults. So 'Mrs' fulfilled all the intentions that the modern Ms has only complicated, and was particularly useful for Mrs Manley, who married into her own surname.

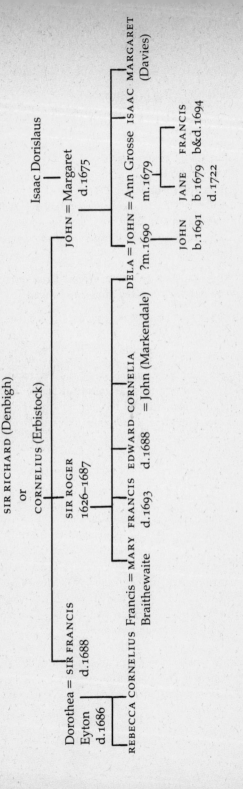

The Manley Family Tree

Introduction

*I first came upon the autobiographical writings of Mrs Delarivier Manley
in my research for* The Female Wits. *So much larger than life do they read
that I was unsurprised when dependable reference works dismissed them as
pure fiction.*

*'The testimony of Mrs Manley is of course wholly valueless,' thought a
nineteenth-century scholar. This century Winston S. Churchill described
her works as 'the lying inventions of a prurient and filthy underworld,
served up to those who relish them and paid for by party interest and political malice'. A late professor of English Literature at Stanford University
expanded the point: 'It is not only that they are repulsive because of the
undisguised licentiousness that everywhere prevails in them; they are
occasionally disgusting on account of the large part played by the merely
horrible.' Mrs Manley, he believed, stood out 'among the least attractive
products of an age of low ideals and scandalous living'. He found her work
'desperately dull and tiresome', despite 'the pornographic horrors of its
pages'.*[1]

*The misogyny implicit in criticism of Mrs Manley comes in various
forms. The most common is one about which she complained throughout
her life – the double standard. She is criticized for achievements which in a
man would have been acceptable and even laudable:* The Cambridge
History of English Literature *informs us that Mrs Manley 'achieved an
unenviable reputation as a novelist', while* The Oxford Companion to
English Literature *boldly states that she 'fell into disreputable courses,
and avenged herself on society for an unhappy life by her New Atalantis'.
'Her subsequent career was one of highly dubious morality but considerable literary success,' the* Dictionary of Literary Biography *grudgingly
admits, while the author of* The Women Novelists *smugly asserts that
she 'wrote novels of some vigour, but deservedly forgotten'. A contributor*

to Notes and Queries *calls her 'this demi-rep – to give her a name exactly as much above her deserts as it is below those of an honest woman.'*[2]

Winston Churchill, whose judgement was utterly partial (so upset did he feel at Mrs Manley's revelations about his great-great-great-great-great-great-great grandfather), agreed: 'The depths of insult are plumbed by the notorious Mrs Manley ... [who] was at this time living with the printer of the Examiner. *She was thus in close touch with Swift ... who used her to write obscenities and insults beyond the wide limits which he set himself.' (Note how he chose to describe her as Swift's printer's mistress rather than admit she was Swift's partner on the* Examiner *– and had in fact introduced the two men to each other.)*[3]

Given this modern critical agreement, my first plans for this book were for an objective biography, backing up the main facts of her life, while exposing an underlying tissue of lies and exaggeration in her autobiography. Surprisingly, the facts proved to be, on the whole, more outrageous than Mrs Manley's fictionalized accounts, and the supporting evidence creates a detective trail which leads right back to her own version. So it seemed more sensible to assemble her autobiographical fragments (which appear in sections varying in length and style in a handful of books which are all unavailable to a wider reading public) in chronological order and write alongside, backing her up and filling in the gaps.

The first obvious question was – who was this woman whose work, though centuries old, drove the British wartime leader to such antipathetic eloquence and language as strong as any he used against Hitler?

What rapidly became clear was that during her own lifetime, and the century following it, political and personal grievances aside, she was widely read and well loved.

The 1699 edition of Langbaine's Lives and Characters of the English Dramatic Poets *encouraged her early work. 'This lady has very happily distinguished herself from the rest of her sex and gives us a living proof of what we might reasonably expect from womankind if they had the benefit of those artificial improvements of learning the men have, when by mere force of nature they so much excel ... There is a force and a fire in her tragedy that is the soul that gives it life and for want of which most of our modern tragedies are heavy, languid, unmoving and dull. In her comedy there is an easy freedom of adding [action?] which confesses a conversation in the authoress no less genteel and entertaining.'*[4]

The Poetical Register *of 1719 thought that 'in all her writings ... there appears a happy sprightliness and an easy turn' and that she herself was 'deservedly esteemed for her affability, wit and loyalty'.*[5]

The Historical Register, *in reporting her death, described her as 'a person of polite genius and uncommon capacity which made her writings naturally delicate and easy and her conversation agreeably entertaining'. And the next year, the unspeakable Curll, bookseller, printer and hack, and not a man to miss any opportunity to exploit a person's frailties, particularly if they could not answer back, wrote this of the 'inimitable author':*

> *All who had the happiness of her conversation were soon convinced how free she was from the general frailties of her sex; what a nobleness and generosity of temper she possessed; how distant her views from the least appearance of self-interest or mean design. How often have I heard her compassionately regretting the miseries of mankind and never her own, but when they prevented her extensive charity to others.*
>
> *Never was she vindictive against the most inveterate enemy; the innate softness of her soul rendered her deportment equally obliging to friends and foes and never did she resent but with the strictest justice.*[6]

Swift's most quoted remark about her is that she was 'very homely and very fat'. He also wrote in his Journal to Stella, *'Got a set of* Examiners, *and five pamphlets, which I have either written or contributed to, except the best, which is the Vindication of the Duke of Marlborough; and is entirely of the author of the Atalantis' and his actions (employing her as an 'understrapper', letting her take over editorship of the* Examiner *and seconding her appeals to the Tories for remuneration for her services) speak louder than his words.*[7]

In 1741 she was described as 'a lady of distinguished merit, whose works will be prized whilst eloquence, wit and good sense are in esteem among mankind ... It seems almost needless to mention the lady's name – not one of the fair sex being at that time so much in vogue for these [qualities] as Mrs Manley.'[8]

Alexander Pope, back in 1712, thought that Mrs Manley's work would be remembered for a very long time. In The Rape of the Lock *he used the phrase 'As long as* Atalantis *shall be read' as a yardstick for eternity.*[9]

It is easy to see the influence Mrs Manley's work had on Swift (particularly Gulliver's Travels*), Richardson, Sterne, Smollett and many others.*

This is not to say that in her own time her work was universally popular. She was a Tory, and therefore not best beloved by the Whigs. Also, like the subjects of William Hickey or Hedda Hopper this century, those who had suffered at the end of her pen squealed very loud.

Delarivier Manley described herself as 'the only person of her sex that knows how to live' and live she certainly did. The daughter of a cavalier, brought up, with her brothers and sisters, in an army camp, she went on to become one of the most feared political satirists – the author of the most sensational bestseller of the eighteenth century, Secret Memoirs . . . from the New Atalantis, and by the time of her death had produced at least twenty-one books and six plays, and been editor of and contributor to two thrice-weekly periodicals, the Female Tatler and the Examiner.

Her work was popular and controversial. Her early success inspired a stage lampoon at her expense. Her Secret Memoirs . . . from the New Atalantis was read by everyone from lords, ladies and politicians to the lowest country bumpkins. It also provoked satires and insults in response and led to her imprisonment.

Of her four known lovers three were lawyers, two of them were MPs, one of them ran a London prison, one owned two theatres and one was a City alderman who went on to become Lord Mayor of London. All four were unscrupulous. Another questionable relationship was with a multi-titled ex-royal-mistress.

Given all this ready-made subject matter, Mrs Manley did not hesitate to use it. She wrote a full-length autobiographical novel, The Adventures of Rivella, under a conveniently male pseudonym, Sir Charles Lovemore. And in her other novels, nestling alongside her fictionalized tales of the rich and famous, she provided us with accounts of incidents in her life not covered in Rivella.

It is important to understand that all of Mrs Manley's autobiographical writing was intended to be read as fiction. She made no attempt at either serious factual biography or humorous, anecdotal self-sketches. The incidents she covers are written in a variety of typical eighteenth-century fiction styles: romantic self-pity, urbane dialogues, letters to distant friends, and all the characters within them are given romantic pseudonyms: Hilaria, Vainlove, Don Marcus and Monsieur L'Ingrat.

Delarivier Manley's taste for the romantic and dramatic was well known and frequently satirized, but in her autobiographical sketches (as in her social and political exposés), although she may have embroidered and elevated, she never evaded the truth of her situation, and the personality which bursts through the often high-flown prose is warm, witty, loyal, trusting and mischievously outspoken.

Her sense of humour was of the raised eyebrow variety. She delighted in the foibles, eccentricity and blind stupidity of others and, while exposing folly, generally showed a warm understanding of it.

Her scandals were not the saucy open-air variety of Chaucer, but, rather, the intense hot-house gropings of men and women (not necessarily in heterosexual couplings) whose appetites went further than the desires of the flesh. Mrs Manley enjoyed exposing sexual intrigue for what it really was – the quest for political or social advancement and greed for money or power.

Such greed in the Churchill ancestor, John, Duke of Marlborough, made him one of her favourite targets and, with Swift, she helped to bring about both John's and his wife Sarah's downfalls. The latest scholarship shows that most of her accusations were firmly based on fact. She exposed among other things his need for perpetual war to keep his personal income high, and the very foundation of his rise to power – the financial help and political preferment earned by his services in the bed of Barbara Villiers, Countess of Castlemaine, and mistress at the time to King Charles II.

Although her work frequently described such scenes complete with languishing bodies undergoing ravishment in jasmine-strewn beds, occasionally she stood back to deliver an analysis of her principal subject – Love:

Of all those passions which may be said to tyrannize over the heart of man, love is not only the most violent, but the most persuasive. It conducts us through storms, tempests, seas, mountains and precipices with as little terror to the mind and as much ease as though through beautiful gardens and delightful meadows.

A lover esteems nothing difficult in pursuit of his desires. It is then that fame, honour, chastity and glory have no longer their due estimation, even in the most virtuous breast. When love truly seizes the heart it is like a malignant fever which thence disperses itself through all the sensible parts. The poison preys upon the vitals and is only extinguished by death or, by as fatal a cure, the accomplishment of its own desires.[10]

And the point was not always made with such typically Baroque cynicism. She sometimes dissected love with an almost Jacobean disdain.

Coquetry may make the fair ridiculous, but love can only make her wretched; that infectious distemper of the heart that poisons all the noble faculties, deludes the sense of glory, degenerates the taste of virtue and by degrees lays the very remembrance of all things but itself into a lethargic slumber.

Let the tender sex suppress the very first suspicion of inclination that sway 'em to a liking of one more than another: if they stay but till that suspicion be confirmed they stay too long, it will be too late to retreat; neither can all its delights be in the least an equivalent for honour lost.

The best that can be said of love is that 'tis a fading sweetness, mixed with bitter passions; a lasting misery chequered with a few momentary pleasures! Love gives the thoughts eyes to see to penetrate everywhere, and ears to the heart to listen with anxiety after all things tho' never so minute. 'Tis bred by permitting themselves leave to desire, nursed by a lazy indulgence to delight, weaned (after strong endeavours and much uneasiness) by jealousy, killed by dissembling and buried, never more to rise, by ingratitude![11]

When delivering talks on Mrs Manley and her sister playwrights in The Female Wits, *I have been accused of dwelling unnecessarily upon their love-lives. Like me, Mrs Manley had an almost obsessive interest in other people's affairs, and often compared people's methods of getting what they wanted in the bedroom with their methods of getting what they wanted in the eighteenth-century version of the boardroom.*

She devoted a large part of her biography to her own affairs, and the pattern which stands out is one which is evident in the lives of many people I know (especially women): Solitude – boredom – work – fame – attractiveness – love – hiatus in work – loss of attractiveness – rejection in love and work – solitude – boredom – work – etcetera. In her professional life she was fearlessly outspoken and strong; in her home life a warm-hearted vulnerable innocent.

The way that love inspired her work but drained her of the energy to execute it is a timeless problem for creative women.

The authors of Pamela's Daughters *pointed out that 'Mrs Manley competed creditably with the best of men and won applause from the most vitriolic of them all, Dean Swift himself . . . She had a heart of oak and the skin of a rhinoceros; no vituperation or reprisal could stop her.' She certainly had extraordinary india-rubber qualities and, whatever got her down, whether personal tragedy or public insult, she bounced back with the swashbuckling energy of an eighteenth-century Joan Collins at the centre of the London literary* Dynasty.[12]

Dolores Duff thought that Swift and Mrs Manley had much in common: 'their minds possessed a coarseness which enabled them to examine and portray the disgusting in a disgusting fashion. Their convictions made them prize honesty and loath hypocrisy; their natural fastidiousness as well as their developed tastes made both almost obsessively concerned with physical cleanliness and decorum.'[13]

Their method of washing other people's dirty linen in public is one still in popular use today. But the exposés of Private Eye and the tabloid gossip columns have neither the wit nor literary grace of Mrs Manley's. Even so, they can still be very effective, as a handful of ex-cabinet ministers could tell you.

A delicate genius, a liar, a wit, a pornographer, an unenviable success, a slut, a failure or, as her good friend Dean Swift said, a woman of generous principles with 'a great deal of sense and invention',[14] *Mrs Delarivier Manley has always been the subject of passionate opinions, but in her autobiography she is the subject of her own passionate opinion, a far more pleasant arrangement.*

1 R. Brook Aspland, *Notes and Queries* 46, 2nd series, November 1856; *Marlborough, his Life and Times*, 1938, I, 132; W. H. Hudson, *Idle Hours in a Library*, 1897, pp. 152, 126, 154
2 *Cambridge History of English Literature*, concise ed., 1970, p. 357; *Oxford Companion to English Literature*, 4th ed., p. 512; *Dictionary of Literary Biography*, 1972, p. 448; R. Brimsley Johnson, *The Women Novelists*, 1918, p. 5; 4 October 1856, ii, 40
3 Winston S. Churchill, *Marlborough, His Life and Times* IV, p. 367
4 *The Lives and Characters of the English Dramatic Poets*, p. 90
5 Giles Jacob, pp. 167, 169
6 *Historical Register* IX, 1724, p. 35; Introduction to 'A Stagecoach Journey to Exeter', 1725. No page numbers
7 *Journal to Stella*, Letter XL, 28 January 1712; Letter XXXII, 22 October 1711
8 *Life and Character of John Barber*, printed T. Cooper, p. 10
9 *The Rape of the Lock*, canto iii, line 165
10 *The Power of Love*, 1720, p. 1
11 *New Atalantis II*, 1709, p. 219
12 Gwendolyn B. Needham and Utter, *Pamela's Daughters*, 1937, p. 37
13 'Materials towards a biography of Mary de la Riviere Manley', dissertation, Indiana 1965, p. 166
14 *Journal to Stella*, Letter XL, 28 January 1712

Prologue

THE ADVENTURES OF RIVELLA
pages 1–14

In one of those fine evenings that are so rarely to be found in England, the young Chevalier D'Aumont, related to the Duke of that name, was taking the air in Somerset House Garden and enjoying the cool breeze from the river, which, after the hottest day that had been known that summer, proved very refreshing. He had made an intimacy with Sir Charles Lovemore, a person of admirable good sense and knowledge and who was now walking in the garden with him, when D'Aumont, leaning over the wall, pleased with observing the rays of the setting sun upon the Thames, changed the discourse.

'Dear Lovemore,' says the Chevalier, 'now the ambassador is engaged elsewhere what hinders me to have the entire command of this garden? If you think it a proper time to perform your promise, I will command the door-keepers that they suffer none to enter here this evening to disturb our conversation.'

Sir Charles having agreed to the proposal and orders being accordingly given, young D'Aumont re-assumed the discourse.

'Condemn not my curiosity,' said he, 'when it puts me upon enquiring after the ingenious women of your nation.'

The gentlemen's conversation first extols the charms of Madame Dacier, a French woman 'without either youth or beauty, yet who makes a thousand conquests, and preserves them too'. Her secret is not some mysterious sexual practice, but those powerful charms, wit, sense and learned conversation.

The subject of witty women leads them through the Duchesse de

Mazarin, the outrageous bi-sexual mistress of Charles II, to the 'famous author of the Atalantis', *Mrs Delarivier Manley herself, under the pseudonym 'Rivella'.*

D'Aumont, intrigued, asks Lovemore to oblige him with as many particulars relating to her life and behaviour as he can possibly recollect.

By this time, the two cavaliers were near one of the benches, upon which reposing themselves, Sir Charles Lovemore, who perceived young D'Aumont was prepared with the utmost attention to hearken to what he should speak, began his discourse in this manner:—

'There are so many things praise and yet blameworthy in Rivella's conduct that, as her friend, I know not well how with a good grace to repeat or, as yours, to conceal, because you seem to expect from me an impartial history.

Her virtues are her own, her vices occasioned by her misfortunes, and yet, as I have often heard her say, if she had been a man she had been without fault. But the charter of that sex being much more confined than ours, what is not a crime in men is scandalous and unpardonable in woman, as she herself has very well observed in divers places throughout her own writings.

Her person is neither tall nor short. From her youth she was inclined to fat, whence I have often heard her flatterers liken her to the Grecian Venus. It is certain, considering that disadvantage, she has the most easy air that one can have. Her hair is of a pale ash colour, fine and in a large quantity. I have heard her friends lament the disaster of her having had the small-pox in such an injurious manner, being a beautiful child before that distemper, but, as that disease has now left her face, she has scarce any pretence to it. Few who have only beheld her in public could be brought to like her, whereas none that became acquainted with her could refrain from loving her.

I have heard several wives and mistresses accuse her of fascination. They would neither trust their husbands, lovers, sons nor brothers with her acquaintance upon terms of the greatest advantage.'

'Speak to me of her eyes,' interrupted the Chevalier. 'You seem to have forgot that index of the mind. Is there to be found in them store of those animating fires with which her writings are filled? Do her eyes love as well as her pen?'

'You reprove me very justly,' answered the baronet, 'Rivella would have a good deal of reason to complain of me if I should silently pass over the best feature in her face. In a word, you have yourself described them. Nothing can be more tender, ingenious and brilliant, with a mixture so languishing and sweet when love is the subject of the discourse, that, without being severe, we may very well conclude the softer passions have their predominancy in her soul.'

'How are her teeth and lips?' spoke the Chevalier. 'Forgive me, dear Lovemore, for breaking in so often upon your discourse, but kissing being the sweetest leading pleasure, 'tis impossible a woman can charm without a good mouth.'

'Yet,' answered Lovemore, 'I have seen very great beauties please, as the common witticism speaks, in spite of their teeth. I do not find but love in the general is well-natured and civil, willing to compound for some defects, since he knows that 'tis very difficult and rare to find true symmetry and all perfections in one person. Red hair, out mouth, thin and livid lips, black, broken teeth, course ugly hands, long thumbs, ill-formed dirty nails, flat, or very large breasts, splay feet, which together makes a frightful composition, yet divided amongst several, prove no allay to the strongest passions.

'But, to do Rivella justice, till she grew fat, there was not, I believe, any defect to be found in her body. Her lips admirably coloured, her teeth small and even, her breath always sweet, her complexion fair and fresh. Yet with all this you must be used to her before she can be thought thoroughly agreeable. Her hands and arms have been publicly celebrated, it is certain that I never saw any so well-turned. Her neck and breasts have an established reputation for beauty and colour. Her feet small and pretty.

'Thus I have run through whatever custom suffers to be visible to us, and, upon my word, Chevalier, I never saw any of Rivella's hidden charms.'

'Pardon me this once,' said D'Aumont, 'and I assure you, dear Sir Charles, I will not hastily interrupt you again. What humour is she of? Is her manner gay or serious? Has she wit in her conversation as well as her pen?'

'What do you call wit?' answered Lovemore. 'If by that word you mean a succession of such things as can bear repetition, even down to posterity, how few are there of such persons, or, rather, none indeed that can be always witty! Rivella speaks things pleasantly. Her company is entertaining to the last. No woman except one's mistress wearies one so little as herself. Her knowledge is universal. She discourses well and agreeably upon all subjects, bating a little affectation, which nevertheless becomes her admirably well. Yet this thing is to be commended in her, that she rarely speaks of her own writings unless when she would expressly ask the judgement of her friends, insomuch that I was well pleased at the character a certain person gave her (who did not mean it much to her advantage) that one might discourse seven years together with Rivella and never find out from herself that she was a wit or an author.'

'I have one pardon more to ask you,' cried the Chevalier, in a manner that fully accused himself for breach of promise. 'Is she genteel?'

'She is easy,' answered his friend, 'which is as much as can be expected from the embonpoint. Her person is always nicely clean and her garb fashionable.'

'What we say in respect of the fair sex I find goes for little,' pursued the Chevalier. 'I'll change my promise of silence with your leave, Sir Charles, into conditions of interrupting you whenever I am more than ordinarily pleased with what you say, and therefore do now begin with telling you that I find myself resolved to be in love with Rivella. I easily forgive want of beauty in her face to the charms you tell me are in her person. I hope there are no hideous vices in her mind to deform the fair idea you have given me of fine hands and arms, a beautiful neck and breast, pretty feet and, I take it for granted, limbs that make up the symmetry of the whole.'

'Rivella is certainly much indebted,' continued Lovemore, 'to a liberal education and those early precepts of virtue taught her and practised in her father's house. There was then such a foundation laid, that, though youth, misfortunes and love for several years have interrupted so fair a building, yet, some time since, she is returned with the greatest application to repair that loss and defect, if not with relation to this world, where women have found it impossible to be reinstated, yet of the next, which has mercifully told us: mankind can commit no crimes but what upon conversion may be forgiven.

'Rivella's natural temper is haughty, impatient of contradiction. She is nicely tenacious of the privilege of her own sex in point of what respect ought to be paid by ours to the ladies, and, as she understands good breeding to a punctuality, though the freedom of her humour often dispenses with forms, she will not easily forgive what person soever shall be wanting in that which custom has made her due.

'Her soul is soft and tender to the afflicted, her tears wait upon their misfortunes and there is nothing she does not do to assuage them. You need but tell her a person is in misery to engage her concern, her purse and her interest in their behalf. I have often heard her say that she was an utter stranger to what is meant by hatred and revenge, nor was she ever known to pursue hers upon any person though often injured (excepting Mr Steele, whose notorious ingratitude and breach of friendship affected her too far and made her think it the highest piece of justice to expose him).

'Now I have done with her person I fear you will think me too particular in my description of her mind. But, Chevalier, there lies the intrinsic value, 'tis that which either accomplishes or deforms a person. I will in few words conclude her character. She has loved expense even to being extravagant, which in a woman of fortune might more justly have been termed generosity. She is grateful, unalterable in those principles of loyalty derived from her family; a little too vainglorious of those perfections which have been ascribed to her.

'She does not however boast of what praise or favours persons of rank may have conferred upon her. She loves truth, and has too often given herself the liberty to speak as well as write it.'

1

First Love

THE ADVENTURES OF RIVELLA
pages 14–29

She was born in Hampshire, in one of those islands which formerly belonged to France, where her father was governor.

Afterwards he enjoyed the same post in other places in England. He was the second son of an ancient family. The better part of the estate was ruined in the Civil War by adhering to the royal family without ever being repaired or scarce taken notice of at the Restoration. The governor was brave, full of honour and a very fine gentleman. He became a scholar in the midst of a camp, having left the university at sixteen years of age to follow the fortunes of King Charles the First.

His temper had too much of the stoic in it for the good of his family. After a life, the best part spent in civil and foreign war, he began to love ease and retirement, devoting himself to his study and the charge of his post, without ever following the Court. His great virtue and modesty rendered him unfit for soliciting such persons by whom preference was to be gained, so that his deserts seemed buried and forgotten. In his solitude he wrote several tracts for his own amusement. His Latin commentaries of the civil wars of England, having passed through Europe, may perhaps have reached your notice, which is all that I shall mention to you of his writings, because you are unacquainted with our English state of learning. And yet, upon recollection, since *The Turkish Spy* has been translated into other languages, I must likewise tell you that our governor was the genuine author of the first volume of that admired and successful work.

An ingenious physician, related to the family by marriage, had the charge of looking over his papers amongst which he found that manuscript, which he easily reserved to his proper use, and both by his own pen and the assistance of some others, continued the work until the eighth volume, without ever having the justice to name the author of the first.

But this is little relating to the adventures of Delarivier, who had the misfortune to be born with an indifferent beauty, between two sisters perfectly handsome. And yet, as I have often thought myself, and as I have heard others say, they had less power over mankind than had Delarivier. Mary, the eldest, was unhappily bestowed in marriage (at her own request, by her father's fondness and assent to his daughter's choice) on a wretch every way unworthy of her, of her fortune, her birth, her charms or tenderness. The eldest was now upon her marriage. Cornelia, the youngest, scarce yet thought of.

Delarivier had just reached the age of twelve, when I beheld the wonderful effects of love upon the heart of young and innocent persons. I had used to please myself in taking romantic stories to her and with furnishing her with books of that strain.

The fair Mary was six years elder, and above my hopes. I was a mere lad, as yet unfashioned. I beheld her with admiration, as we do a glorious sky: it is not yet our hemisphere, nor do we think of shining there. Delarivier was nearer to my age and understanding, and though four years younger than myself, was the wittiest girl in the world. I would have kissed her and embraced her a thousand times over, but had no opportunity.

Never any young ladies had so severe an education. They had lost their mother when very young, and their father, who had passed many years abroad during the exile of the royal family, had brought into England with him all the jealousy and distrust of the Spaniard and Italian. I have often heard Delarivier regret her having never gone to school, as losing the innocent play and diversions of those of her own age. A severe governante, worse than any duenna, forbid all approaches to the apartment of the fair. As young as I was, I could only be admitted at dinner or supper when our family visited, but never alone.

She was fond of scribbling, though in so tender an age. She wrote verses, which, considering her youth, were pardonable, since they might be read without disgust, but there was something surprising in her letters, so natural, so spirituous, so sprightly, so well turned, that, from the first to the last, I must, and ever will, maintain that all her productions, however successful they have been, come short of her talent in writing letters. I have had numbers of them. My servants used to wait on her as if to bring her books to read, in the cover of which I had contrived always to send her a note, which she returned in the same manner.

But this was perfect fooling. I loved her, but she did not return my passion. Yet without any affected coyness, or personating a heroine of the many romances she daily read, Delarivier would let me know in the very best language, with a bewitching air of sincerity and manners, that she was not really cruel, but insensible, that I had hitherto failed of inspiring her with new thoughts, since her young heart was not conscious of any alteration in my favour but, in return to that generous concern I expressed for her, she would instruct it as much as possible to be grateful, till when my letters and the pleasure of writing to me again was a diversion more to her taste than any she met with besides and therefore would not deny herself the satisfaction of hearing from, or from answering, me as often as she had an opportunity.

But all my hopes of touching her heart were suddenly blasted. To bring myself back to what I was just now telling you of the strange effects of love in youthful hearts, I must acquaint you that upon the report of an invasion from Holland, a supply of forces was sent to the garrison, amongst which was a subaltern officer, the most beautiful youth I remember to have ever seen... This young fellow ... had no other pretences but those of his person to qualify him for being my rival, neither of himself did he dream of becoming such. He durst not presume to lift up his eyes to the favourite daughter of the governor but, alas, hers descended to fix themselves on him. I have heard her to declare since that, though she had read so much of love and that I had often spoke to her of it in my letters, yet she was utterly ignorant of what it was, till she felt his fatal power, nay, after she had felt it she scarce guessed at her disease till she found a cure.

Young Carlisle, for so was my rival called, knew not how to receive a good fortune which was to become so obvious that even her father and all the company perceived her distemper better than herself. Her eyes were continually fixed on this young warrior. She could neither eat nor sleep. She became hectic, and had all the symptoms of a dangerous indisposition. They caused her to be let blood, which, joined to her abstinence from food, made her but the weaker, whilst the distemper grew more strong.

The gentleman who had newly married her sister was of counsel with the family how to suppress this growing misfortune. He spoke roundly to the youth, who had no thoughts of improving the opportunity, and charged him not to give in to the follies of the young girl. He told him he would shoot him through the head if he attempted anything towards soothing Delarivier's prepossession or, rather, madness.

Carlisle, who was passionately in love elsewhere, easily assured them he had no designs upon that very young lady, and would decline all opportunities of entertaining her. But as the governor's hospitable table made most persons welcome, he forbore not to pursue his first invitation and came to dinner, where the dear little creature saw him constantly, and never moved her eyes from his face.

His voice was very good, the songs then in vogue amorous and such as suited her temper of mind. She drank the poison both at her ears and eyes, and never took care to manage or conceal her passion. Possibly what she has since told me in that point was true; that she knew not what she did, as not having free will or the benefit of reflection, nor could she consider anything but Carlisle, though amidst a crowd.

The governor was a wise man, and forbore saying anything to the girl which might acquaint her with her own distemper, much less cause her to suspect that himself and the others were acquainted with it. He caressed her more than usual, soothed and lamented her indisposition, proposed change of air to her. She fell a-weeping and begged she might not go to be sick from under his care, for that would certainly break her heart. He thought gentle methods were the best and therefore ordered her sisters and their governess to do all they could to divert, but never to leave her alone with the young Carlisle. In the meantime, by the interest the governor had at Court, he procured that battalion to be recalled and another to be deputed in place of what had given him so much uneasiness.

The day before their marching orders came, he proposed play-

ing after dinner for an hour or two at hazard.* Most of the gentlemen present were willing to entertain the governor. Carlisle
excused himself as having lost the last night all his small stock at
backgammon. His little mistress heard this with a vast concern
and, as she afterwards told me, could have readily bestowed upon
him all she had of value in the world. Her father, who beheld her
in a deep reverie, with her eyes fixed intently upon Carlisle, called
her to him and, giving her a key where his money was kept, ordered her to fetch him a certain sum to play with. She obeyed, but
no sooner beheld the glittering store (without reflecting on what
might be the consequence, or indeed anything else but that her
dear Carlisle wanted money) than she dipped her little hand into
an hundred pound bag full of guineas, and drew thence as much
as it would hold. Upon her return she met him in the gallery.
(Seeing the company engaged in play, he was stolen off, possibly
with an intent to follow Delarivier and have a moment to speak to
her in without witnesses for the regard he gave her from his eyes
when he durst encounter hers spoke him willing to be grateful.)
She bid him hold out his hat and say nothing, then, throwing in
the spoil, she briskly passed on to the company, brought her
father the money he wanted, returned him the key, and set herself
down to overlook the gamesters.

This story I have had from herself, by which action she was since
convinced of the greatness of her prepossession, being perfectly
just by nature, principle and education, nothing but love, and that
in a high degree, could have made her otherwise. The awe she was
in of her father was so great that upon the highest emergency she
would not, durst not, have wronged him of a single shilling.
Whether the governor never missed those guineas, as having
always a great deal of money by him for the garrison's subsistence,
or that he was too wise to speak of a thing that would have reflected upon his daughter's credit, Delarivier was so happy as to hear
no more of it.

Meantime my affair went on but ill. She answered none of my
letters, nay, forgot to read them. When I came to visit her she
showed me a pocketful which she had never opened. This vexed
me excessively, and the more when she suffered me with extreme
indifference to take them again. I would have known the reason of

Hazard: a dice game from which the modern American game of 'craps' is
  derived.

this alteration. She could not account for it, so that I left her with outward rage, but inwardly my heart was more her slave than before; whether it be the vile and sordid nature of the god of love to make us mostly dote upon ungenerous usage and, at other times, to cause us to return with equal ingratitude the kindness we meet from others.

The next day I engaged my sister to make a visit to the castle. We took the cool of the morning. She was intimate with Mary before her marriage, and suffered herself to be persuaded to let me wait on her.

We were drinking chocolate in the governor's toilet,* where Delarivier and her sisters attended, when the drums beat a loud alarm. We were presently told we should see a very fine sight: the new forces march in, and the old ones out – if they can properly be called so, that had not been there above eighteen days. At the news, my mistress, who had heard nothing of it before, began to turn pale as death. She ran to her Papa and, falling upon his bosom, wept and sobbed with such vehemence that he apprehended she was falling into hysteric fits. Her father sent for her governess to carry her to her bedchamber, but she hung upon him in such a manner that, without doing her a great deal of violence, they could not remove her thence. I ran to her assistance with a wonder great as my concern, but she more particularly rejected my touches and all that I could say for her consolation.

Meantime the Commander-in-Chief, followed by most of his officers (amongst which the lovely Carlisle appeared with a languishing air full of disappointment, which yet added to his beauty), came up to the governor and told him his men were all under arms and ready to march forth whenever he pleased to give the word of command. At the same time entered another gentleman, equally attended, whom the governor stepped forth to welcome. He assured him the forces that obeyed him were all drawn up on the counterscarp and thought themselves happy, more particularly himself, to have the good fortune of being quartered where a person of such honour and humanity was governor.

To conclude, poor Delarivier fell from one fainting into another, without the least immodest expression, glance or discovery of what had occasioned her fright. She was removed and we had the

*Toilet: a small dressing room.

satisfaction of seeing the military change of forces and poor Carlisle depart without ever beholding his mistress more . . .

Delarivier recovered and begged she might be removed for some time to any other place which would better agree with her than the air wherein I breathed. In a word, without ever having been beloved, my importunities now caused me to be for some time even hated by her.

The lady had a younger brother who was pensioned at a Huguenot minister's house on the other side of the sea and country, about eighteen miles farther from London, a solitude rude and barbarous. Delarivier begged to be sent thither that she might improve time and learn French. She would not have any servant with her for fear of talking English. Nor would she ever speak to her brother in that language.

What shall I say? So incredible was her application, though she had a relapse of her former distemper, that in three months' time she was instructed so far as to read, speak and write French with a perfection truly wonderful, insomuch that when her father came to take her home, finding the air had very much impaired her health, the good minister, her master, who was a learned and modest person, begged the governor to leave mademoiselle with him, and he would engage in twelve months, counting from the time she first came, to make her mistress of those four languages of which he was master, viz: Latin, French, Spanish and Italian.

The next day after her return I came to pay my duty to her and welcome her back. She was less averse, but not more tender. My sisters tattling with her sisters had gained the secret, and, very little to my ease, imparted the confidence to me. We began an habit of friendship on her side, though on mine it never ceased to be love . . .

After this short absence I found myself condemned to a more lasting one. My father designed to send me abroad with an intent that I might spend some years in my travel. At the same time Delarivier had the promise of the next vacancy for maid of honour to the Queen. I congratulated her good fortune, acquainting her with my ill fortune in being condemned to separate myself from her.

Though I was never happy in her love, yet I was jealous of losing her friendship amidst the diversions of a Court and the dangers of absence . . . I begged her to secure to me by a marriage unknown to our parents, but I could not prevail with her. She feared to

35

displease her father, and I durst not ask the consent of mine. I had flattered myself that it was much easier to gain their pardon than procure their approbation, because we were both so young. But Delarivier was immovable, notwithstanding all that I could say to her . . . I departed for Italy.

The abdication immediately came on. The Queen was gone to France and Delarivier thereby disappointed of going to Court.

Her father was what he termed himself, truly loyal. He layed down his command and retired with his family to a private life and a small country house, where the misfortunes of his royal master sunk so deep into his thoughts that he died soon after in mortal apprehension of what would befall his unhappy country.

Here begin Delarivier's real misfortunes. It would be well for her that I could say here she died with honour, as did her father.

THE FACTS

Manley is indeed an ancient family name. Burke's Landed Gentry claims that the Manleys came over with William the Conqueror and were named in the Roll of Battle Abbey. However, modern scholarship on the Roll considers that the reference is to Mauley rather than Manley, which is an old English name.[1]

This branch of the Manley family came from Denbighshire and Sir Roger was the second son of either Sir Richard Manley of Denbigh or Cornelius Manley of Erbistock (most probably the latter). Traditionally royalist, he fought for the King in the Civil War, serving in the garrison of Denbigh, which surrendered to Parliament in 1645.[2] *Like many Cavaliers, when in 1648 the King's fate seemed certain, he went into exile in Holland until the Restoration of King Charles II in 1660. He was certainly back in England by 1665 when he was commissioned as an ensign in the Holland Regiment.*[3]

Surprisingly, Sir Roger's younger brother, John, fought in the Cromwellian army. It is possible that he was influenced by his wife's family as Margaret Manley was the daughter of Isaac Dorislaus, the Dutch diplomat who was assassinated in 1649 by twelve exiled royalists for his part in the execution of King Charles.

Sir Roger became a scholar in the years spent in foreign exile during the Commonwealth, and kept up his writing and translating until his death. His published works include A True Description of the Mighty Kingdoms of Japan and Siam, *written originally in Dutch by Francis Caron and Joost Schorten, and now rendered into English by Captain Roger Manley (1663),* The History of the late Warrs in Denmark *(1670),* Commentariorum de Rebellione Anglicana *(1686) and a continuation of* The Turkish History *(1687) by Richard Knolles and Sir Paul Rycaut. It is possible that Mrs Manley confused this last work with* The Turkish Spy *which is generally ascribed to Giovanni Paolo Marana.*

He received his knighthood for services to the crown, but the story of the restoration of the monarchy is one of rewards promised and promises unfulfilled.

Delarivier Manley's claim to have been 'born in Hampshire, in one of those islands which formerly belonged to France, where her father was governor' has a lot to support it. Although there is no baptismal record (the parish registers in the Channel Islands have suffered worse than most), there is strong circumstantial evidence.

From 1667 to 1672 her father, Sir Roger Manley, was stationed in the Channel Islands. In October 1667 he was made lieutenant-governor (under Sir Thomas Morgan) and commander of all His Majesty's castles, forts and forces within the island of Jersey.[4]

A son, Roger, who must have been the eldest boy (assuming the customary naming of the first son after the father), was baptized on 18 September 1672 at Grouville. So, allowing for the gestation period, Delarivier Manley cannot have been born between January 1672 and June 1673. Her date of birth, if born while her father was in Jersey, must have been between 1667 and 1671.

After his stint in Jersey he served as a Captain of the Royal Regiment of Foot Guards at Windsor, Tower Hamlets, briefly in Brussels and finally in Portsmouth, from where in February 1680, he and his family (sons Francis and Edward, and daughters Mary Elizabeth, Delarivier and Cornelia; presumably his wife and son Roger were dead by this time – there is no mention of either of them in either Sir Roger's or Edward's wills) moved to Landguard Fort in Suffolk, where he was made governor.[5]

Captain Francis Braithewaite, who became Mary Elizabeth Manley's husband, came to Landguard Fort, with the Twelfth, or Suffolk, Regiment on 11 July 1685, and returned to Yarmouth on 3 August 1685.[6]

In Braithewaite's regiment was a young ensign, James Carlisle. After such a sheltered upbringing, Mrs Manley's attraction to Carlisle is understandable. He had been an actor with the United Company, and presumably had picked up a few of those eyes-and-teeth tricks so successful with adolescent girls. In 1682 he had joined the Drury Lane Theatre company, and *was described as one of the younger players after these manoeuvres in 1687. His play* The Fortune Hunters *was performed at Drury Lane in 1689.*

In a country so frequently at war as England in the late seventeenth century it was quite routine for men to serve in the armed services between jobs, and Carlisle returned to his army career to meet his death at the battle of Aughrim on 12 July 1691.[7]

As unlikely as Mrs Manley's version seems, her exaggeration about the regiment's short stay under her father's command is not excessive, for the Twelfth Regiment was stationed at Landguard Fort for only 24 days.[8]

The events following her infatuation with Carlisle were very fortunate for her future career as a writer. It was fairly customary to send boys to Europe for part of their education, but Mrs Manley's stay in France was much more than girls of her time could have hoped for. Later evidence proves that she was indeed fluent in French by 1691.

It was, however, more usual for girls of her age and class to do a stint at court. Mrs Manley was disappointed because the Queen, Mary of Modena, fled the country when anti-Catholic feeling reached its peak in December 1688.

The dates at about this time begin to become slightly muddled, although of course Mrs Manley's version makes for a better story. Sir Roger had acquired a 'small country house' at Kew in Surrey, but his death predates the revolution, and he died in harness, for Lt-Col. Eyton became governor of Landguard Fort in place of 'Sir Roger Manley, deceased' on the 19 March 1687.[9]

1 *Burke's Landed Gentry II*, 1889, p. 1055. Roll of Battle Abbey
2 S. R. Gardiner, *The History of the Great Civil War*, London, 1893, IV, p. 201
3 *War Office Commission Book 1660–1684*, p. 70
4 J. H. Leslie, *The History of Landguard Fort*, London, 1898, p. 100
5 'Domestic Entry Book', vol. 29, p. 351
6 Charles Dalton, 'English Army Lists 1661–1714', London, 1892–1904, II, p. 33; E. A. H. Webb, *History of the 12th Regiment 1685–1913*, London 1914, pp. 3–4. Archives of the Grenadier Guards
7 Dalton, II, p. 33; W. Van Lennep, *The London Stage 1660–1800*, Carbondale, 1965, I, pp. 370, 385; P. H. Highfill Jr et al., *A Biographical Dictionary of Actors, Actresses, Musicians in London 1660–1800*, 1973–
8 E. A. H. Webb, pp. 3–4
9 PROB/11, piece 391; 'Calendar of State Papers, Domestic series, Jan 1686–May 1687'

2

Married, Possessed and Ruined

From the elegant conversation of Sir Charles Lovemore and his friend the Chevalier D'Aumont, in the gardens of Somerset House, Mrs Manley sweeps us to the illustrious Palace of Beaumond, where the spirits Astraea and Intelligence listen in on Delia (alias Mrs Manley) sobbing out her story.

NEW ATALANTIS II
pages 182–91

My father had, indeed, a military employment, which, though not half of the value of that paternal estate which was lavished in the royal service, yet upon his decease we were sensible of the loss of it. He left behind him three daughters and a son; my brother was killed in his marine command in the late war under William III's government.

Thus all the support we had remaining fell in the defence of an ungrateful people, who never consider the unhappy relics of a family, desolate and neglected, never extend their regards to those who remain monuments of their injustice, though their misfortune and ruin have no other foundation than the loyalty of their ancestors, their contempt of life and an honourable, nay, glorious, loss of it in defence of their gods and of their country. What then can remain with their ruined offspring, but stubborn discontent, heart burnings and complaint of their undoing?

Neither was a brother of my father's (though by an error of education made of the factious party) more fortunate. He had considerably enriched himself, but purchasing a wrong title upon

39

the Restoration of the royal line it reverted back to the former possessor, so that he was left with several small children, an unpitied example of rebellion.

To the eldest of these my father took care to give the education of a gentleman, and endeavoured to tincture him with true principles. He loved him with a distinguishing tenderness, something that he could not have for his own children because they were too young for that reasonable part of conversation which he met in John Manley. To him it was that, upon his dying bed, he left the care of my youngest sister and myself (the eldest having much the advantage of us in age was married and gone off with a husband so ill-natured and disobliging that our family no longer conversed with theirs).

My father associated with John Manley two remote relations. One immediately after died, the other was old, had gained a large estate in the world, lived at the distance of above two hundred miles from us, loved his ease, and resolved to enjoy it, so that he left the care of us and our affairs wholly in John Manley's hands.

He had always had an obliging fondness that was wonderfully taking with girls. We loved him as much as it was possible.

He sent us into the country to an old out-of-fashion aunt, full of the heroic stiffness of her own times, would read us books of chivalry and romances with her spectacles. This sort of conversation infected me and made me fancy every stranger that I saw, in what habit soever, some disguised prince or lover.

It was not long before my aunt died and left us at large without any control.

This immediately reached John Manley's notice. He took post and came down to fetch us to London. He was in deep mourning, as he told us, for his wife. We congratulated with him for his deliverance from an old, uneasy lady that we remembered enough of to hate ever since we had been children. She had buried herself for many years in the country, a vast distance from London, so that none of our family retained any correspondence with theirs.

My cousin-guardian immediately declared himself my lover with such an eagerness that none can guess at who are not acquainted with the violence of his temper. I was no otherwise pleased with it than as he had answered something to the character I had found in those books that had poisoned and deluded my dawning reason. However, I had the honour and cruelty of a true heroine and would not permit my adorer so much as a kiss from my hand without ten thousand times more entreaty than anything of that nature could be worth.

But, not to dwell upon such trifles, I fell ill of a violent fever where my life was despaired of.

John Manley and my sister never quitted the chamber in sixteen nights, nor took any repose than by throwing themselves alternately upon the little pallet in the same room. In short, having ever had a gratitude in my nature, and a tender set of benefits, upon my recovery I promised to marry him.

'Twas fatally for me performed in the presence of my sister, one maid-servant and a gentleman who had married a relation of ours. I was then wanting of fourteen, without any deceit or guess at it in others.

'Tis true I had formerly heard John Manley's lady repeat, in the violence of her rage, the base methods he had took to gain her, producing writings to a good estate when he had but the expectations of a small one and that not till after the death of his father. I should not urge this particular against him, but to acquaint you that mine was not his first deceit. His lady is still, for ought I know, a living witness of the truth of this. To sum it all in a little, I was married, possessed and ruined.

He brought me to London and fixed me in a remote quarter of it, forbade me to stir out of doors, or to receive the visits of my friends or acquaintance. I thought this a very rough proceeding and grieved the more excessively at it since I had married him only because I thought he loved me.

Those who know his person will easily believe that I was not in love with him. He was about two or three and twenty years older than I was, and, as I have often heard him say himself, a man and with my father in the next chamber when I was born.

Then as to his person: his face and shape had never been handsome. What he values himself upon most is his sort of an out-of-the-way blustering wit, by no means polite. You know him vain, talkative, opinionated, mixing a thousand absurdities with every grain of sense. Then, so perfect a libertine that he never denied himself the gratifications of any of his passions, every way a debauchee. Yet can this man talk of honour, of loyalty, of losing all for his duty, though wholly forgetful of it, when he joined William with Monmouth securing the strongest citadel of the kingdom against the reigning prince, and naming it the Glorious Cause.

But not succeeding in his first pretensions (where he put in for being one of the divan*) he revolted back to the royal party and made himself all that reign a distinguishing, noisy tool, only fit to speak there what the men of discretion of his side were well enough contented to hear.

Neither could interest be said to move me. Unless his wife were dead I must find him a beggar. She had a pretty estate, but her daughter was to have it and, whilst she was living, I could not pretend to the use of any share of it. This may suffice against the ill-natured part of the world, who, when my misfortune began to be public (for I was the last to know about it) were so malicious to say that either I was never married or else no stranger to his lady's being alive. The latter part I have sufficiently answered by the little inducement I could have from his person or circumstances. And as to the first, my sister and servant are both alive and witnesses of my marriage. The gentleman indeed is dead, but it was not without all the detestation imaginable at being made a party in the deceit. Doubtless he had called John Manley to a severe account but that my prayers and entreaties, tender of bloodshed, deferred that revenge which, soon after, his death prevented him from pursuing.

I was uneasy at being kept a prisoner, but my husband's fondness and jealousy was the pretence. I had always loved reading, to which I was now more than ever obliged, or much of my time had hung upon my hands. Soon after, I proved with child, and so perpetually ill that I implored John Manley to let me have the company of my sister and my friends. When he could have no relief from my importunity (being assured that in seeing my relations I should learn the more than barbarous deceit he had used to betray me), he thought that it was best for himself to discover it.

After having first tried all the arguments he could invent, then the authority of a husband, but in vain, for I was fixed to my point and would have my sister's company, he fell upon his knees before me with so much confusion, distress and anguish that I was at a loss to know what could work him to such a pitch.

At length, with a thousand interrupting tears and sobs, he stabbed me with the wounding relation of his wife's being still alive, conjured me to have some mercy upon a lost man, as he was,

*Divan: Council of State.

42

in an obstinate, inveterate passion, that had no alternative but death or possession, could he have supported the pain of living without me, he would never have made himself so great a villain. But, when the absolute question was whether he should shoot himself or betray me, self-love had turned the balance, though not without that anguish to his soul as had poisoned all his delights, having a thousand times started in his guilty sleep, my father's form perpetually haunting his troubled dreams, reproaching him as a traitor to that trust which in the pangs of death he had reposed in him and, as a double villain, casting an impure, an indelible stain upon the honour of a family which was so nearly his own, representing to his tortured imagination all the expense and care he had of his education, more like a father than an uncle, for which he had so ungratefully rewarded him in the ruin of his daughter, who but for him might have flourished fair, an ornament to his house, at least not a reproach to it.

My rising grief forbids me to dwell upon so distressful a subject, or on half those accusations with which John Manley cunningly loaded himself to be beforehand in those he expected I should make him.

But alas, my surprise and grief were beyond the ease of words, beyond the benefit of tears. Horror, amazement, sense of honour lost, the world's opinion, ten thousand distresses crowded my wounded imagination! I cast my looks upon the conscious traitor with horrible dismay. The stubborn tears refused to flow to my relief. I could not sigh, I could not groan, my blood was stagnated, so was my reason. He carried me to the bed all motionless. Oh, that some pitying god had that moment tore me from his impious embraces, that I had had but strength or courage to have abandoned the villain, to have left him to perpetual remorse, to the never-ending invasions of his own conscience! Oh, that I had but then proclaimed him through all the streets of London for the betrayer of my glory, the destroyer of an ancient, worthy family which had never (in their women) had a stain. Then I had probably secured myself from the reproach of being a conscious partner to my own undoing. Oh, unexperienced youth! Oh, unavailing reason, why is it that you never appear in an age that has most occasion for you? . . .

Alas, what relief was there for me? My brother that might have revenged my wrongs was newly killed at sea. The nearest relation of a man was him, the traitor that had seduced me to ruin by a specious pretence.

My fortune was in his hands, or worse, already lavished away in those excesses of drinking and play that he could not abstain from though he had lately married me, a wife whom he pretended to be fond of.

I was young, unacquainted with the world, had never seen the necessities of it, knew no arts, had not been exposed to any hard-ships. My father, a man of true honour and principles, nicely just in his affairs with all the world, lived in a handsome manner and so I had been educated.

What could I do? Forlorn! Distressed! Beggared! To whom could I run for revenge, even from want and misery, but to the very traitor that had undone me? I was acquainted with none that would espouse my cause, a helpless, useless load of grief and melancholy. With child! Disgraced! My own relations either impo-tent of power or will to relieve me!

Thus was I detained by my unhappy circumstances and his pre-vailing arts to wear away three wretched years in his guilty house, though no entreaty, no persuasion, could ever again reconcile me to his impious arms, conscious to myself of having there done my duty whatever appearance my living with him had as to the world.

My wretched son, whenever I cast my eyes upon him, was a mortal wound to my repose. The errors of his birth glared full upon my imagination. I saw the future upbraiding him with his father's treachery and his mother's misfortunes.

Thus forsaking, and forsaken of all the world, in the morn of life, whilst all things should have been gay and promising, I wore away three wretched years without either one companion or acquaint-ance. As my reason increased, so did my sense of honour lost. I began vainly to consider whether it was an impossible attempt to retrieve it.

John Manley had lately got a considerable employment. The duties of it obliged him to go into the country where his first wife lived. He took a tender farewell of me, and promised a due care of myself and child, said he would now endeavour to do me justice in my fortune, and save the greatest part of his new income to repair the wastes that he had made, persuaded me to have gone with him into the country, and, to seduce or quiet my conscience, showed me a famed piece that was newly wrote in defence of polygamy and concubinage, by one who was after Lord Chancellor.

When he was gone he soon relapsed into his former extravagances and unworthily left me to repine and complain at his neglect and barbarity, happy only in being released from the killing anguish of every day having before my eyes the object of my undoing.

When, by degrees, I began to look abroad in the world, I found the reputation I had lost by living in such a clandestine manner with John Manley had destroyed all the esteem that my truth and conversation might have else procured me. Oh, nice, unrelenting glory, is it impossible to retrieve thee, impossible to bend thee? Wilt thou forever be inexorable and ingrateful to my caresses? Is there no retrieve for honour lost? The gracious gods, more merciful to the sins of mortals, accept repentance, though the nobler part, the soul, be there concerned and suffer our sins to be washed away by tears of penitence. But the world, truly inexorable, is never reconciled. Unequal distribution! Why are your sex so partially distinguished? Why is it in your powers, after accumulated crimes, to regain opinion, when ours, though oftentimes guilty but in appearance, are irretrievably lost? Can no regularity of behaviour reconcile us? Is it not this inhospitality that brings so many unhappy wretches to destruction, despairing of redemption, from one vile degree to another they plunge themselves down to the lowest ebb of infamy?

THE FACTS

There is a slight ambiguity in Mrs Manley's list of surviving siblings. In 1687 four were alive. Her brother Edward died in June 1688 and was buried 'in woollen' in St Michael's Bassishaw.[1] Mary Elizabeth was married to the disliked Braithewaite, and inherited her father's house at Kew. It is possible that the family's antipathy stemmed from the fact that Braithewaite was a Catholic (he resigned his commission on the accession of William and Mary).

Francis became lieutenant of the York *on 11 October 1688, and was promoted to command of the fireship* Roebuck *in January 1691. In 1693 he was promoted to Captain of the* Swan *or* Sun Prize, *a twenty-four gun* sixth rate on mackerel fishery protection in the North Sea. On 15 June the ship was taken by the French after a brave defence. Francis Manley was wounded and taken prisoner. He died in France two days later.[2]

Sir Roger Manley nominated Ellis Lloyd and William Eyton, 'dear friends and kinsmen', as executors of his will. These could be the 'remote relations'. There are papers linking the Erbistock families of Manley, Eyton and Lloyd which date back to 1614.[3] In his will Edward Manley described Edward Lloyd (Ellis's father) as his 'loving uncle'.[4]

William Eyton succeeded Sir Roger as governor of Landguard Fort, and was related to Dorothea Manley, née Eyton, Sir Roger's sister-in-law. Lloyd died in 1687, Eyton in January 1688.[5]

Sir Roger's elder brother, Sir Francis Manley, a Welsh judge, who lived in Erbistock, near Wrexham ('a distance above two hundred miles'), also qualifies. The 'old out-of-fashion aunt' has previously been identified as Sir Francis's wife, Lady Dorothea Manley, but this cannot be so as Lady Dorothea was buried on 10 July 1686.[6] Sir Francis died soon after his brother, and this left John Manley as their next of kin. (Possibly, the aunt was John Manley senior's second wife, Mary.)

Son of the Cromwellian major (who was MP for Denbighshire boroughs and for Bridport from 1689 to 1694) and nephew of Sir Roger, John Manley enrolled at Gray's Inn on 4 November 1671. (Gray's Inn was obviously a family tradition. Francis and his son Cornelius Manley had enrolled before him, and Ellis Lloyd was a contemporary.)[7]

John Manley junior was a Tory, unlike his father, which strengthens Mrs Manley's story that Sir Roger had raised John as though he was his own son. He was employed as a lawyer by John Granville, first Earl of Bath, the Tory lord-lieutenant of Devon and Cornwall, who pledged his support for William of Orange on 19 November 1688, very early in William's march to London and the crown. 'The strongest citadel in the kingdom' was presumably Plymouth which William secured with the help of the Granvilles.

In 1689 he contested the seat at Truro, where he had a successful legal practice, but was not seated in the house. He followed this up with quite a successful career in politics, becoming MP for Bossiney 1695–1707, Camelford 1708–9, and Bossiney again in 1710, until his death in 1713.

John Manley married Anne Grosse, a Cornish heiress, 'her parents dead', at Westminster Abbey, on 19 January 1678/9. He was aged 'about 24', she was 'about 23' and brought with her substantial property in Truro as well as a large lump sum.[8]

Delarivier Manley must have been born between 1670 and 1678 (see

Appendix) in which case John would certainly have been 'a man' at the time.

Before marrying John Manley she 'fell ill of a violent fever', possibly the smallpox she refers to in the Prologue (p. 25).

There are two children recorded as John and Anne Manley's: a daughter, Jane, christened in Truro on 25 August 1680, and fourteen years later, a son, Francis, christened 9 August and buried in December 1694.[9]

In between these legitimate children he had another son, John, christened on 13 July 1691 in the parish of St Martin-in-the-Fields, Westminster, of 'John and Dela Manley'. The child was born nineteen days earlier on the 24 June. John Manley was 36 and had been married to his first wife Anne Manley for thirteen years.

Westminster, where John must have lived with Dela, was very convenient for his work in Parliament House and the King's Bench Courts which were both situated in Westminster Hall, and was, in 1690–1, a remote, although busy, quarter of London.

John Manley does not seem to have been a very pleasant man. Mrs Manley's opinion of him was understandably low. Jonathan Swift described him as 'a beast'. He was sent to the Tower for insolence in the House of Commons, and described by a fellow MP as 'a silly hot fellow'. In January 1706 he was involved in an incident with another Cornish MP, Thomas Dodson, and was wounded in the arm. Dodson was run through the body but reported 'like to recover'.[10]

His friend, the Lord Chancellor who advocated bigamy, was William Cowper, Lord Chancellor from 1705 to 1710. Like John Manley, he was both a lawyer and MP. It was popularly believed that he seduced Elizabeth Culling by means of a sham marriage[11] *(Bishop Nicolson's diary refers to Cowper's 'other wife'). Voltaire's* Dictionnaire philosophique *(1764) states that Cowper was the author of a treatise for polygamy, but the source of this could possibly be Mrs Manley. Swift insinuates that Cowper was a bigamist in* Examiner *17 and 22.*

1 *Parish Register*, St Michael's Bassishaw, 1943, II, p. 130
2 Calendar of State Papers, Domestic series, 1699–1700, p. 329; W. Laird Clowes, *The Royal Navy – A History*, II, 1897, p. 472; John Charnock, *Biographia Navalis*, II, 1795, pp. 400–1
3 PROB 11/391 f. 291; 'The Manley Papers' (1457–1719), for sale at Howard and Heirloom Ltd in March 1981
4 PROB 11/391 f. 293

5 J. H. Leslie, *The History of Landguard Fort*, p. 101
6 Wrexham Parish Registers Jul. 10, 1686
7 J. Foster, *Register of Admissions to Gray's Inn 1521–1889*, 1889, pp. 313, 235, 307
8 J. Foster, *London Marriage Licences*, London, 1889, p. 879; G. Armytage, *Allegations for Marriage licences*, Westminster, 1886, p. 291
9 Register of St Mary's Truro, I, pp. 228, 243
10 *History of Parliament Trust*; Luttrell, *A Brief Historical Relation of State Affairs*, VI, p. 535
11 Kippis, *Biographia Britannica*, IV, p. 389

3

Lady Castlemaine, the Royal Mistress

Sir Charles Lovemore resumes his version of the life of Mrs Manley . . .

THE ADVENTURES OF RIVELLA
pages 29–41

I was almost a year in the search and then gave it over, till one night I happened to call in at Madam Mazarin's, where I saw Delarivier introduced by Lady Castlemaine, a royal mistress of one of our preceding kings. I shook my head in beholding her in such company . . .

She was much impaired. Her sprightly air, in which lay her greatest charm, was turned into a languishing melancholy, the white of her skin degenerated into a yellowish hue, occasioned by her misfortunes and three years' solitude (though quickly after she recovered both her air and her complexion).

How confused and abashed she was at my addressing to her! The freedom of the place gave me opportunity to say what I pleased to her. She was not one of the gamesters, but begged me I would be pleased to retire and spare her the shame of an eclaircissement in a place no way proper for such an affair. I obeyed and accepted the offer she made me of supping with her at Lady Castlemaine's house, where at present she was lodged, that lady having seldom the power of returning home from play before morning unless upon a very ill run when she chanced to lose her money sooner than ordinary . . .

She told me all her misfortunes with an air so perfectly ingenuous that if some part of the world who were not acquainted with

49

her virtue ridiculed her marriage and the villainy of her kinsman, I, who knew her sincerity, could not help believing all she said. My tears were witnesses of my grief. It was not in my power to say anything to lessen hers. I therefore left her abruptly, without being able to eat or drink anything with her for that night.

Time, which allays all our passions, lessened the sorrow I felt for Delarivier's ruin, and even made me an advocate to assuage hers. The diversions of the house she was in were dangerous restoratives. Her wit and gaiety of temper returned, but not her innocence.

Lady Castlemaine had met with Delarivier in her solitary mansion, visiting a lady who lived next door to the poor recluse.*

She was the only person that in three years Delarivier had conversed with, and that but since her husband was gone into the country. Her story was quickly known.

Lady Castlemaine, passionately fond of new faces of which sex soever, used a thousand arguments to dissuade her from wearing away her bloom in grief and solitude. She read her a learned lecture upon the ill-nature of the world that would never restore a woman's reputation, how innocent soever she really were, if appearances proved to be against her. Therefore she gave her advice, which she did not disdain to practise, the English of which was: to make herself as happy as she could without valuing or regretting those by whom it was impossible to be valued.

The lady at whose house Delarivier first became acquainted with Lady Castlemaine perceived her indiscretion in bringing them together. The love of novelty as usual so far prevailed that herself was immediately discarded, and Delarivier persuaded to take up her residence near Lady Castlemaine's, which made her so inveterate an enemy to Delarivier that the first great blow struck against her reputation proceeded from that woman's malicious tongue. She was not contented to tell all persons who began to know and esteem Delarivier that her marriage was a cheat, but even sent letters by the penny-post to make Lady Castlemaine jealous of Delarivier's youth in respect of him who at that time happened to be her favourite.

Delarivier has often told me that from Lady Castlemaine she received the first ill impressions of John Churchill, touching his in-

*According to Mrs Manley's *Key to Rivella*, her London neighbour was Mrs Elizabeth Ryder, daughter of Sir Richard Fanshaw, the scholar and diplomat.

gratitude, immorality and avarice, being herself an eyewitness when he denied Lady Castlemaine (who had given him thousands) the common civility of lending her twenty guineas at bassett,* which, together with betraying his master and raising himself by his sister's dishonour, she had always esteemed a just and flaming subject for satire.

Delarivier had now reigned six months in Lady Castlemaine's favour (an age to one of her inconstant temper) when that lady found out a new face to whom the old must give place, and such a one of whom she could not justly have any jealousy in point of youth or agreeableness. The person I speak of was a kitchen-maid† married to her master who had been refuged with King James in France.

He died and left her what he had, which was quickly squandered at play, but she gained experience enough by it to make gaming her livelihood, and returned into England with the monstrous affectation of calling herself a Frenchwoman, her dialect being thenceforward nothing but a sort of broken English. This passed upon the town because her original was so obscure that they were unacquainted with it. She generally plied at Madam Mazarin's bassett table and was also of use to her in affairs of pleasure, but whether that lady grew weary of her impertinence and strange ridiculous airs, or that she thought Lady Castlemaine might prove a better bubble, she profited of the advances that were made her and accepted an invitation to come and take up her lodging at Lady Castlemaine's house, where in a few months she repaid the civility that had been shown her by clapping up a clandestine match between her patroness's eldest son, a person though of weak intellects yet of great consideration, and a young lady of little or no fortune.

But, to return to Delarivier, Lady Castlemaine was tired and resolved to take the first opportunity to be rude to her. She knew her spirit would not easily forgive any point of incivility or disrespect.

Lady Castlemaine was querulous, fierce, loquacious, excessively fond or infamously rude. When she was disgusted with any person she never failed to reproach them with all the bitterness and wit she was mistress of, with such malice and ill-nature that

*Bassett: a card game which went through a craze, particularly among women, at the turn of the seventeeth/eighteenth centuries.
†'... pretended Madam Beauclair ...' in Key to Rivella.

she was hated not only by all the world but by her own children and family. Not one of her servants but would have laughed to see her lie dead amongst them, how affecting soever such objects are in any other case. The extremes of prodigality and covetousness, of love and hatred, of dotage and aversion were joined together in Lady Castlemaine's soul.

Delarivier may well call it her second great misfortune to have been acquainted with that lady who, to excuse her own inconstancy, always blasted the character of those whom she was grown weary of, as if by slander and scandal she could take the odium from herself and fix it upon others.

Some few days before Lady Castlemaine was resolved to part with Delarivier to make room for the person who was to succeed her, she pretended a more than ordinary passion caused her to quit her lodgings to come and take part of her own bed. Delarivier attributed this feint of kindness to the lady's fears lest she should see the man Lady Castlemaine was in love with at more ease in her own house than when she was in hers, though that beloved person had always a hatred and distrust of Delarivier.

He kept a mistress in the next street in as much grandeur as his lady. He feared she would come to the knowledge of it by this new and young favourite, whose birth and temper put her above the hopes of bringing her into his interest, as he took care all others should be that approached Lady Castlemaine. He resolved, how dishonourable soever the procedure were, to ruin Delarivier, for fear she should ruin him, and therefore told his lady she had made advances to him, which, for her ladyship's sake, he had rejected. This agreed with the unknown intelligence that had been sent by the penny-post. But, because she was not yet provided with any lady that would be her favourite in Delarivier's place, she took no notice of her fears but politically chose to give her a great and lovely amusement. It was with one of her own sons, whom she caressed more than usual to draw him oftener to her house, leaving them together upon such plausible pretences as seemed the effect of accident not design. What might have proceeded from so dangerous a temptation I dare not presume to determine because Lady Castlemaine and Delarivier's friendship immediately broke off upon the assurance the former had received from the broken-Frenchwoman that she would come and supply her place.

The last day she was at Lady Castlemaine's house, just as they sat down to dinner, Delarivier was told that her sister Mary's husband was fallen into great distress which so sensibly affected her that she could eat nothing. She sent word to a friend who could give her an account of the whole matter, that she would wait upon her at six o'clock at night, resolving not to lose that post if it were true that her sister was in misfortune, without sending her some relief.

After dinner several ladies came in to cards. Lady Castlemaine asked Delarivier to play. She begged her ladyship's excuse because she had business at six o'clock. They persuaded her to play for two hours, which accordingly she did, and then had a coach sent for and returned not till eight.

She had been informed abroad that matters were very well composed touching her sister's affairs, which extremely lightened her heart. She came back in a very good humour and very hungry, which she told Lady Castlemaine, who, with the leave of the first duchess in England, that was then at play, ordered supper to be immediately got ready for that her dear Delarivier had eat nothing all day.

As soon as they were set to table Delarivier repeated those words again, that she was very hungry. Lady Castlemaine told her she was glad of it, there were some things which got one a good stomach. Delarivier asked her ladyship what those things were. Lady Castlemaine answered, 'Don't you know what? That which you have been doing with my – ', and named her own son. 'Nay, don't blush, Delarivier, 'twas doubtless an appointment. I saw him today kiss you as he lead you through the dark drawing room down to dinner.'

'Your ladyship may have seen him attempt it,' answered Delarivier, perfectly frighted with her words, 'and seen me refuse the honour.'

'But why', replied Castlemaine, 'did you go out in a hackney coach* without a servant?'

'Because', says Delarivier, 'my visit lay a great way off, too far for your ladyship's chairmen to go. It rained, and does still rain extremely. I was tender of your ladyship's horses this cold, wet night. Both the footmen were gone on errands. I asked below for one of them. I was too well mannered to take the black and leave none to attend your ladyship, especially when my lady duchess

---

Hackney coach: a hired coach. It would have seemed odd that Mrs Manley chose to travel in one when Lady Castlemaine obviously had her own coaches.

was here. Besides, your own porter paid the coachman, which was the same I carried out with me. He was forced to wait for some time at the gate till a guinea could be changed, because I had no silver. I beg all this good company to judge whether any woman would be so indiscreet, knowing very well, as I do, that I have one friend in this house that would not fail examining the coachman where he had carried me, if it were but in hopes of doing me a prejudice with the world and your ladyship.'

The truth is, Lady Castlemaine was always superstitious at play. She won whilst Delarivier was there, and would not have her removed from the place she was in, thinking she brought her good luck.

After she was gone her luck turned, so that before Delarivier came back Lady Castlemaine had lost above two hundred guineas, which put her into a humour to expose Delarivier in the manner you have heard; who briskly rose up from the table without eating anything, begging her ladyship's leave to retire, whom she knew to be so great a mistress of sense, as well as good manners, that she would never have affronted any person at her own table but one whom she held unworthy of the honour of sitting there.

Next morning she wrote a note to Lady Castlemaine's son to desire the favour of seeing him. He accordingly obeyed. Delarivier desired him to acquaint my lady where he was last night from six till eight. He told her at the play in the side box with the Duke of —, whom he would bring to justify what he said. I chanced to come in to drink tea with the ladies. Delarivier told me her distress. I was moved at it and the more because I had been myself at the play and saw the person for whom she was accused sit the play out. In a word, Delarivier waited till Lady Castlemaine was visible and then went to take her leave of her with such an air of resentment, innocence yet good manners as quite confounded the haughty Lady Castlemaine.

But I, who knew Delarivier's innocency, begged she would retire to my seat in the country where she might be sure to command with the same power, as if it were her own, as in effect it must be, since myself was so devoted to her service. I made her this offer because it could no longer do her an injury in the opinion of the world which was sufficiently prejudiced against her already. She excused herself, upon telling me she must first be in love with a man before she thought fit to reside with him, which was not my case, though she had never failed in respect, esteem and friend-ship for me. She told me her love of solitude was improved by her disgust of the world, and since it was impossible for her to be public with reputation, she was resolved to remain in it concealed. She was sorry that the war hindered her to go into France, where she had a very great inclination to pass her days, but since that could not be helped she said her design was to waste most of her time in England in places where she was unknown.

To be short, she spent two years in this amusement. In all that time never making herself acquainted at any place where she lived.

THE FACTS

Mrs Manley's landlady, Barbara Villiers, Duchess of Cleveland, Countess of Southampton, Baroness Nonsuch and Countess of Castle-maine was born in 1641 of low-ranking aristocratic parents. In 1659 she married Roger Palmer, a commoner, and shortly afterwards elevated her-self by sleeping with the King, Charles II.

In exchange for services rendered Charles made Mrs Palmer lady of the bedchamber to his wife, Catherine, and showered her with titles, properties and profitable gifts: wine licences, leases, grants and excise revenues as well as the fairytale palace of Nonsuch which she demolished, selling off the materials at a handsome profit and leasing out the plot for a regular income.

Of her six children (three boys, three girls) Charles probably fathered four and lavished gifts and titles on all six. Roger Palmer, her husband, refused to use his title, regarding it as the price of infamy.

Described by Oldmixon as 'the lewdest as well as the fairest of all King Charles's concubines',[1] she was one of the most important figures of the Restoration and in her heyday had considerable power in Court and society.

When Charles's interest began to wane, she also had affairs with the playwright William Wycherley and the young John Churchill (who prob-ably fathered her daughter, Barbara) before she moved to Paris in 1676.

Her exile was partly an attempt to save face over the ascendancy of the King's other mistress, Louise de Kerouaille, Duchess of Portsmouth, but when his latest, Hortense Mancini, Duchesse de Mazarin, arrived dressed as a man, and attended by a multitude of servants and a blackamoor boy, it was the final straw.

One of the famous nieces of Cardinal Mazarin, Madame Mazarin was beautiful, and bi-sexual, with blue-black eyes and hair. After separating from her husband, Charles de la Porte, she made it her business to become a mistress to the voluptuary King of England.

A few months after the Duchesse de Mazarin's arrival and Lady Castlemaine's departure, the Duchesse held a fencing match in Hyde Park with Lady Castlemaine's pregnant daughter, Anne. From Paris Lady Castlemaine wrote a letter of complaint to the King. Anne was sent to Herstmonceux, where she lost the baby, and spent so much time kissing a portrait of the Duchesse that there were fears for both her health and sanity.

When Mrs Manley became Lady Castlemaine's lucky mascot in January 1694 the enmity between the two ex-royal-mistresses had dwindled to presiding over rival gambling tables and poaching each other's 'lucky mascots'. Their King was dead and both women were unpopular in the Court of William and Mary. Both were Catholic, and Lady Castlemaine was £10,000 in debt.

Lady Castlemaine had returned to England shortly before Charles died, and started an affair with 'her favourite', the notorious actor/highwayman, Cardell Goodman.

He carried with him a formidable reputation: he was expelled from Cambridge for defacing the Duke of Monmouth's portrait, deprived of his place as a Page of the Backstairs on a charge of negligence, he had been an apprentice actor in the King's Company since 1673. In the late 1670s, to supplement his income, he started moonlighting – he became a highwayman.

Early in his affair with Lady Castlemaine he was also brought to trial for conspiring to hire Alexander Amadei to poison the Dukes of Grafton and Northumberland (her sons) and fined £1000. The forgiving Countess obtained a royal pardon for his crimes. In return he refused to let any performance begin until her Ladyship was in her seat.

True to Mrs Manley's account, the Countess's son, Charles Fitzroy, Duke of Southampton, married Anne Pulteney in November 1694, five months after Mrs Manley left the Countess's company. It could hardly be described as a good match.

It is probable that during her six months with Lady Castlemaine Delarivier Manley picked up much of the gossip which she later used to contribute to the downfall of John Churchill, first Duke of Marlborough.

Son of an impoverished Royalist, Churchill's first official post was page *to the Duke of York. Once kitted out and with a commission in the Guards, he swiftly rose to the rank of Colonel, and his prospects were considerably enhanced in 1677 by his clandestine marriage to Sarah Jennings, Princess Anne's confidante. His part in suppressing the Monmouth rebellion led to a barony, and his support for William of Orange led eventually to the earldom of Marlborough. He assumed supreme command in the War of Spanish succession and Queen Anne heaped honours and gifts upon him, including an annual stipend of £10,000, the order of the Garter and the Blenheim estate at Woodstock, while his wife flaunted it as Groom of the Stole, Mistress of the Robes, Keeper of the Privy Purse and the Queen's bosom friend.*

However, it had all begun with a douceur of £5000 and an ensigncy in the Guards provided by the doting Countess of Castlemaine (at the time she was openly the King's mistress), and when, in December 1711, the Tories were conspiring for an end to Churchill's European war, they were not above encouraging the gutter journalism of Mrs Manley and her partner Jonathan Swift, who in turn were not above dredging up the sexual foundation of his meteoric career. There is a famous story that King Charles once found Churchill hiding in Lady Castlemaine's drinks cabinet and merely remarked, 'I forgive you, for you do it for your bread.'

Mrs Manley, in a typical passage, describes the seduction by Lady Castlemaine (still at this time not far past her bloom) of Churchill's friend, Henry, Baron Dover. The situation had been set up by Churchill so that he could find his mistress in flagrante delicto and thus, having taken all the money and preferment that Lady Castlemaine had offered, still have a good excuse for dumping her and setting up with the ambitious young Sarah Jennings. This is presumably just a fragment of the material which annoyed his descendant Sir Winston Churchill.

NEW ATALANTIS I
pages 33–4

The Duchess went to the Count's the next day, immediately after she had dined. She scarce allowed herself time to eat, so much more valuable in her sense were the pleasures of love. The servants were all out of the way as usual, only one gentleman that told her his lord was lain down upon a day bed that joined the bathing room, and he believed was fallen asleep since he came out of the bath.

The Duchess softly entered that little chamber of repose; the weather violently hot, the umbrellas were let down from behind the windows, the sashes open and the jessamine that covered 'em blew in with a gentle fragrancy, tuberoses set in pretty gilt and china pots were placed advantageously upon stands, the curtain of the bed drawn back to the canopy made of yellow velvet embroidered with white bugles, the panels of the chamber looking-glass, upon the bed were strowed, with a lavish profuseness, plenty of orange and lemon flowers and, to complete the scene, the young Dover in a dress and posture not very decent to describe.

It was he that was newly risen from the bath and, in a loose gown of carnation taffeta, stained with Indian figures, his beautiful long, flowing hair (for then 'twas the custom to wear their own tied back with a ribbon of the same colour) he had thrown himself upon the bed, pretending to sleep, with nothing on but his shirt and night-gown, which he had so indecently disposed that, slumbering as he appeared, his whole person stood confessed to the eyes of the amorous Duchess. His limbs were exactly formed, his skin shiningly white, and the pleasure the lady's graceful entrance gave him diffused joy and desire throughout all his form. His lovely eyes seemed to be closed, his face turned on one side (to favour the deceit) was obscured by the lace depending from the pillows on which he rested.

The Duchess, who had about her all those desires she expected to employ in the arms of the Count, was so blinded by 'em that at first she did not perceive the mistake, so that giving her eyes time to wander over beauties so inviting and which increased her flame, with an amorous sigh she gently threw herself on the bed close to the desiring youth.

The ribbon of his shirt-neck not tied, the bosom (adorned with the finest lace) was open, upon which she fixed her charming mouth. Impatient, and finding that he did not awake, she raised her head and laid her lips to that part of his face that was revealed.

The burning lover thought it was now time to put an end to his pretended sleep. He clasped her in his arms, grasped her to his bosom; her own desires helped the deceit. She shut her eyes with a languishing sweetness, calling him by intervals 'her dear Count', 'her only lover', taking and giving a thousand kisses. He got the possession of her person with so much transport that she owned all her former enjoyments were imperfect to the pleasure of this.

Delarivier Manley's stay with the loquacious Countess may have been miserable, but it certainly provided her with excellent copy and, in 1705, when Mrs Manley's popularity was high, I am sure she must have enjoyed the irony of their reversal of fortunes. Lady Castlemaine's husband, Roger Palmer (whom she had left in 1662) died, leaving her free to marry Robert 'Beau' Feilding, a man at least ten years her junior. The decrepit Lady Castlemaine shortly discovered that he had married a Mrs Wadsworth only a fortnight before he had married her, and that their marriage was therefore bigamous.

1 *The Critical History of England*, II, 1728–30, p. 270.

4

A Stagecoach Journey to Exeter

With a reputation blemished beyond repair; a 'marriage' to an already married man, a questionable relationship with Lady Castlemaine and whispers of an intrigue with the Lady's son, all compounding the rumour that she is a demi-rep, Mrs Manley decides to get out of town. She takes the stagecoach to the West Country. En route she writes a series of letters to an unknown friend in London.

LETTERS WRITTEN BY MRS MANLEY
1696, pages 1–11, 25–36, 43–48, 58–62,
63–50 (faulty numbering in edition, should be 66)

I
Egham, June 24th, 1694

I am got, as they tell me, sixteen miles from you and London, but I can't help fancying 'tis so many degrees. Though midsummer to all besides, in my breast there's nothing but frozen imaginations. The resolutions I have taken of quitting London (which is as much as to say the world) forever starts back and asks my gayer part if't has well weighed the sense of ever. Nor does your letter, which I received this morning, taking coach, less influence me than when I first formed the design. You should have used but half those arguments and then they had undoubtedly prevailed. 'Tis of the latest now to ask me why I leave the crowded market and retire to starve alone in solitude. Whereas you quote the poet,

All your beauty no more light will have
Than a sun-dial in a grave.

I am too much afraid sloth and sadness are going to be my eternal companions, and you know my soul's unfitted for such guests till upon the road to execution. I fancied dying to the world. Horace, Cowley, all those illustrious lovers of solitude debauched my opinion against my reason.

I took coach with Mr Granville's words in my mouth,

Place me, ye gods, in some obscure retreat.
Oh, keep me innocent, make others great.
In quiet shades, content with rural sports,
Give me a life remote from guilty Court,
Where, free from hopes and fears, at humble ease,
Unheard of, I may live and die in peace.

Yet you see how great a change two hours has produced. All my constancy is not proof against the thought I am going to have no lover but myself for ever.

The green, inviting grass, upon which I promised to pass many pleasing solitary hours, seems not at all entertaining. The trees, with all their blooming, spreading beauties, appear the worst sort of canopy because, where I am going, they can offer their shade to none but solitary me.

But 'tis not reasonable my dullness should extend to you, who have everything in your nature just and pleasing. You asked, and I eagerly engaged, because you desired, to give an account of myself and travels, every stage. I have not forgot when I told you 'twas too often how you answered: not for a mind so fruitful as mine in variety of inconstant thoughts. You find at present they run all upon melancholy apprehensions, which have so solely possessed me, I have not had time to observe my wretched fellow travellers, only a pert sir in the company that will make himself be taken notice of by his dullness.

They most unmercifully set us to dinner at ten o'clock upon a great leg of mutton. 'Tis the custom of these dining stages to prepare one day beef and another our present fare. 'Tis ready against the coach comes. And, though you should have a perfect antipathy, there's no remedy but fasting. The coachman begs your pardon – he'd not stay dressing a dinner for the King, god bless him, should he travel in his coach.

I have left the limb of the sheep to the mercy of my companions, whose stomachs are thus early prepared for any digestion, to tell you, with what unfeigned respect I shall be ever your true, faithful servant.

II
Hartley Row, June 22nd, 1694

I am got safely to Hartley Row, and in a little better humour than when I writ my last.

Our landlord is a perfect beau and most exquisitely performs the honours of his house. I am in pain for his assiduity. I can't fetch a step, no, not from the window, from the table etc. but he is squiring me. And so dressed and so conceited that nothing but serving a loose apprenticeship could have set him up a master in the trade of foppery. He was a goldsmith's apprentice, where he studied more his pleasures than profit. This house fell to him and he wisely resolved to keep it himself with the help of his sister, who is a neat, housewifely, obliging sort of woman. I suppose 'tis by much the best entertainment the road affords.

They have a tolerable cook, and I was glad to see something I could eat at three o'clock, for we came here in at two and I can give you a little better account of my fellow travellers.

The sir I spoke of is a baronet's son, as he has carefully given me to understand. I take it for granted he likes me and would have me do the same by him. As he came in, he put off his travelling suit for a coat and vest designed to dazzle the curate and all his congregation. The way I found to mortify his foppery was not to speak a word of the change, which made him extremely uneasy. At length, out of all patience, he desired my opinion if his tailor had used him well, what the brocade was worth a yard, how many ounces of silver-fringe, and recommended to my curiosity the exquisite workmanship of the loops, and then gave me the sum total of the cost. I answered him that finery was lost upon me, I neither was, nor pretended to be, a judge. He pertly answered he perceived by my sullenness that I had a great deal of wit, though I understood he had but little by his remark.

Well, all this did not do. He would fain have had me enquire into his family, intrigues and fortune, which, when he perceived I had no curiosity for, 'Faith, madam,' said he, 'I beg your lady-ship's opinion if I am not the most unfortunate man breathing. I'll tell you a most mortifying adventure – nay you must hear me – I vow this indifferency does not look natural to you, your eyes promise us much more fire.'

'I'll shut them,' thought I, 'for ever, rather than such a fop shall find anything to like them for.'

'What, no answer, madam?' said he. 'I perceive your attention by your silence. Gad, I love a person of your breeding, that knows themselves better than to interrupt a good story.'

'Perhaps madam is not well with her journey,' answered Mrs Mayoress of Totnes. 'Alas! I wonder riding in the coach should not have given you a better stomach. Poor gentlewoman, she has scarce eat anything.'

'I'll recompense that by a feast of the mind,' answered my fop. 'How say you madam? Shall I begin the regalio?'

'I had as good consent,' quoth I. 'With or without my leave, I see you are resolved upon't.'

'Well then, madam,' said he, 'since you are disposed to be delighted, I'll about it instantly.' . . .

'Tis now past eleven, and they'll call us by two. Good night. I am going to try if I can drown in sleep, that which most sensibly affects me, the cruel separation we have so lately suffered.

III
Sutton, June 23rd, 1694

Don't you think I am more constant than your friendship could hope, or mine pretend to? I think it a great proof of it, amidst the fatigues of a West Country journey, to give you thus daily an account of my insignificant self and travels. We parted from Hart-ley Row at three this morning through a crowd of beggars, who watch your coach for alms, and will never leave it unblessed. Hence my Beau took occasion of simile, bid me to observe how wakeful those wretches were for small charities, that he would do the like in hopes of greater, and that my Divine Idea had so filled his sight he could not resolve to let sleep intrude for fear of shut-ting me out.

I perceived he took pains to be thought uneasy and I have more good manners than to disappoint him.

Mrs Mayoress, now she is acquainted, has all the low, disagreeable familiarity of people of her rank. She entertained us all the morning with a sorry love-business about her second husband, stuff so impertinent I remember nothing of it.

Beau continues his assiduities. I think none was ever so plagued with dying eyes. His are continually in that posture, and my opposites, that I am forced to take a great deal of pains to avoid 'em.

The other two fellow travellers were never so promoted before and are much troubled their journey is to last no longer, and wish the four days four months. I hope every jolt will squash their guts, and give 'em enough on't. But they are proof against any such disasters and hugely delighted with what they are pleased to call 'riding in state'.

After this ridiculous account you need not doubt but I am thoroughly mortified.

The trouts are just brought upon the table, which is the only good thing here. They look inviting and won't stay for cooling compliments. I hope time will show it none to say I am unalterably yours.

IV
Salisbury, Saturday night

I can't give myself any reason why these coachmen are such rogues. They make us rise at two in the morning to bring us into our inn at the same hour in the afternoon. After we were reposed a little, Beau shined again, as yesterday, and waited upon me to evening prayers.

I need say nothing to you of Salisbury Cathedral. If in a foreign country, as the lady in her letters of Spain, I could entertain you with a noble description, but you have either seen, or may see it and so I'll spare my architecture.

There are abundance of pretty, innocent-looked women, genteel enough, but I have lost my heart to a handsome churchman. I never thought before that dress was tolerable but so wore it seems a mighty ornament. He was placed behind me, but I turned my devotion and kneeled to him, imagining him no less than, as in my antique days, some high priest of the sun.

The canon gave me cause to think he had dined too well and was obliged to his snuff, more than religion, for keeping him awake.

Well, devotion done, I was forced to break up mine and leave him without a knowledge of his conquest.

As we were walking to our inn, I asked Beau what we should do to pass the next day without being very weary of each other, for Sunday does not permit travelling. He, you may be sure, did not fail to tell me he could never be weary of me, though himself expiring by my sight and cruelty. I waved his compliment and told him my design of engaging the people in the Exeter coach, if they seemed worth it, to live with us for the time. When we returned we were told it was not yet come in, occasioned by the breaking of the axle-tree five miles off, but that a fellow was gone to mend it and they were expected every moment.

My chamber window answered the court. I rose to it at the noise of the coach, and presently saw alight a tall, blustering, big-boned, raw thing, like an overgrown schoolboy, but conceited above everything. He had an appurtenance called a wife whom he suffered to get out as well as she could. As long as he had lain with her he did not think her worth the civility of his hand. She seemed a giant of a woman, but very fine, with a right cit air. He blustered presently for the best lodgings, which he saw taken up by her that held a fine fan before her face. You may guess this was your humble servant. The chamberlain told him 'twas their custom, first come, first served, but that there were very good chambers besides.

The rest of the company were two things that looked pert and awkward, tradesmen's daughters I judged 'em. But methoughts, casting my eyes upon a gentlewoman and her servant that came out last, I found something pleased me, whether it were because she really deserved it, or that the stuff she was with set her off.

I had a basin of fine heart-cherries before me, just come from the garden. I caused 'em to be brought after me into the gallery, and designed 'em as bait to the woman whom I was to begin the acquaintance with, for Beau designed to set up to get a fortune in Devonshire and was unwilling to show any irregularity and I thought myself above their reflections.

The first that appeared was the wife, with a rising belly. This seemed a good hint. I offered 'em to her, not knowing but she might long. The sight, I suppose did not displease her, for she readily accepted, and ate very greedily. The genteel-looked lady

65

had much to do to be persuaded. As for the other two, they were gone to choose a lodging.

We presently grew acquainted, taking traveller's liberty, and supped together. But shall I tell you? The wife grew jealous of me! It seems her temper was such. And her husband (no small man in his country, though himself just set up in merchandising at London, his father one of the canons at Exeter) thought he might carry all hearts before him, as well as the country lasses. They were coming from visiting their friend and returning to their house in London. Mrs Stanhope, for that was the lady's name that I liked, told me I was not to count on the conquest, for he had given her douceurs all the way and made her extremely uneasy because his wife appeared to be such. We grew into an intimacy and left the company.

My Beau was to me faithless and inconstant. One of the awkward little things I told you of and who had a tolerable face was a goldsmith's daughter of Exeter and acquainted with his lady sister. That began their acquaintance. She seemed free and fond. He took the hint and applied himself to her, which I was very glad of.

Mrs Stanhope went with me to my chamber and, after much discourse, offered friendship and mutual knowledge of each other . . .

The post had just brought me a letter from you. I find you curse me with the continuation of Egham-uneasiness till I return to the world in London. Methinks 'tis unreasonable to impose the continued slavery of writing. I assure you I shall take truce with it till at my journey's end unless something happen worth our notice.

General Tollemache's body was brought in here this evening.

His secretary I am acquainted with and have sent to desire the favour of his company tomorrow to dinner and if anything in his relation be entertaining you shall not fail of it from your sincere, faithful servant.

V

Bridgport, June 25th, 1694

The account of so great a man's death as Mr Tollemache, in the middle of all his enterprises, when fortune seemed to promise him much greener laurels than he had yet gathered, has so added to my melancholy that I will not describe his misfortune to you for fear it be contagious, but rather suffer you to expect the public account, for I am one of those that esteem you more than to make you uneasy, as I think none can be otherwise that hears the particulars of his loss. Something there was extreme touching.

After this doleful subject, methinks my Beau may justly complain I have so long a time neglected his most singular self. We parted this morning from our Sunday-acquaintance. Fop told me, when I greatly reproached him for inconstancy, 'Gad, madam, 'tis but to make myself the newer to your ladyship tomorrow.' I rather thought 'twas to keep me such to him.

He has given me a relation of his success with the damsel. She treated him, in her chamber, with rosa solis* and what he calls sucket.† The rest he would have willingly acquainted me with but I recommended discretion in ladies' affairs and he, almost bursting, is yet forced to be silent. How long he will keep such I do not know, for he has often offered at breaking his most painful penance.

We have passed Dorchester and Blandford today, but nothing I found in either worth your notice.

The toils of the body influence the mind. I suppose by my dullness you find I speak woeful truths.

We are lodged at Bridgport, and very ill, but 'tis but for a night. Here's just come into the inn an acquaintance of Beau's, who promises yielding matter for tomorrow's letter.

This was infected in the beginning by General Tollemache, and the most uneasy journey as dully concludes it.

VI
Exeter, June 26th, 1694

Beau is now grown so insipid that I shall say very little of him for the future, and I have reason to believe myself such to him, for these two last evenings, contrary to custom, he has not re-dressed. The fatigue, which he seems more sensible of than any of us, has tarnished the lustre of his eyes, and instead of any further ogling,

*Rosa solis: fruit liquor.
†Sucket: candied fruit.

drowns all his amorous pretensions in profound sleep as the uneasy jolting of the coach will permit. This is what I can never be so happy to gain . . .

I am now got safely, weary, into Exeter and, I thank god, rid of the impertinency of my fellow travellers, Beau excepted, who will see me safe home, though distant from his.

The cathedral here is very fine. The bishop's seat in it surpasses Salisbury, though short in everything else.

Forgive me for leaving you thus abruptly, since it is more pleasing to entertain myself with a letter of yours just brought to me.

VII
July 10th, 1694

If I have omitted answering your three last, it proceeded from nothing but the desire of doing something new and you know 'tis extremely in me not eagerly to show you all testimonies of friendship.

My solitude is much more pleasing than I fancied it. As yet I am not weary of that happy indifferency which leaves me nothing either to hope or fear.

> Thus empty and thus idle do I live,
> Nor loved, nor loving, can nor take, nor give.

I have most foppish letters from Beau, who parted with a world of seeming regret. And yet I hear he is endeavouring at a mistress. I suppose I may bid his impertinence farewell for ever. I think I bade you hope in one of mine to hear no more of him. I know not how I am fallen upon the nauseous repetition. Themistocles refused Simonides when he would have taught him the art of memory: 'I remember what I would not, but I cannot forget what I would.'

My study has fallen upon religion. I am searching into all sorts. You shall not fail to hear what that chance-medley produces. I can now with cold indifferency shake hands with all things beyond this solitude. How long the extraordinary humour may last I can't inform you at present. I repeat with stoical pride

Keep me, ye bounteous gods, my cave and woods
In peace. Let tares and acorns be my food.

Postscript: I forgot to leave orders with the Jew about the chocolate. Pray take care that it be sent me and excuse this trouble.

VIII
March 15th, 1695

... I think imitation the hardest part of writing. It confines a free-
born genius which naturally loves untrod wilds, at least if I may
guess at another's by my own. And now I am speaking of that, let
me tell you, all those romantic ideas of retirements, which viewed
at a distance gives a ravishing prospect, now I am wedded,
bedded too, prove the worst sort of matrimony. But 'tis only to
such a particular friend as yourself that I dare complain. To the
remoter sort I assume a stoical appetite and air, tell them the world
with all its gaudy pleasures are but rich delusions which at once
corrupts our sense and our fame, that little spot of earth I have
chose to fix my face in has more solid entertainments, more real
innate delights than the glories of Kensington, then sigh and seem
to pity the more elevated part of the world that can bury themselves in noise and crowd.

But, let me tell you, there's no real satisfaction without conversation. I have had so much of the dead since I settled here and, as I
may say, nothing of the living, for I find none deserves the name,
that I wish for the conjuring art and would rather converse with
the ghosts of the departed than always with their books or with
myself ...

Write to me still, but nothing of the news. I mean to hear none
till I see London again, and when that will be I have not the
pleasure so much as to imagine. 'Twill be new to lie forgotten and
forgetting and, as it were, be born with understanding, to all the
vanities and virtues, if any, of that Hydra.

THE FACTS

According to the dedication in the printed edition they were written to J. H., sometimes identified as James Hargreaves, who presumably was responsible for their publication, without the author's permission, timed to coincide with her debut as a London playwright in 1696. Mrs Manley had them withdrawn. The 1725 edition was printed from a copy which the publisher Curll received from Mrs Manley's own hands twenty years before with the 'positive injunction that it should never more see the light till the thread of her life was cut.'[1]

The West country episode, 1694–6, poses an insoluble puzzle. Our information is that she went as far as Exeter in 1694, was still in the country in 1695 and returned to London by 1696. On these facts alone the editors of British Authors before 1800 come to the conclusion that for 'two years Mrs Manley seems to have strayed morally and physically up and down the West of England'.[2]

Considering the emotional high jinks Mrs Manley had been through for about four years her spirits are remarkably high.

The dating of the letters is particularly curious. Her son, John, was born on 24 June 1691. The first letter, from Egham, was written on 21 June 1694, but dated 'June 24th'. Three days later, from Salisbury, when it was 24 June, Mrs Manley omits the date altogether and dates the letter only 'Saturday'. It is of course possible that the misdating was a genuine oversight, however it is not beyond the realms of imagination to suppose that the 24 June, the birthday of her abandoned son, would be a traumatic date.

There are two possibilities of the whereabouts of her son at this time: either John Manley had confessed to his wife, Anne, and the child was in Truro, or Delarivier Manley was attempting to look after him herself – a difficult task for a young woman with no income. The child was certainly alive, as in 1698 John Manley proposed to his cousin-wife a method of gaining money from the Albemarle estates for their son.[3]

Mrs Manley's destination, some distance further than Exeter, which was the end of the line on the stagecoach, points towards Cornwall; Cornwall points to Truro and her cousin-husband.

Now that Mrs Manley was no longer under the financial care of Lady Castlemaine, John Manley, who had 'promised a due care' of Delarivier Manley and her child, would be her only hope of a living. Perhaps her presence in the vicinity of his real wife would pressurize him sufficiently to give her the promised maintenance; perhaps he had the child (John) and motherly interest brought Mrs Manley down; or perhaps she had kept the child, and now came down to dump it on its father's doorstep.

Another possibility (and with Mrs Manley the most illogical is often the case) is that she simply went there to while away her time in solitude.

Her father, Sir Roger, had applied for the office of Receiver General of Cornwall when he had been in his post at Landguard Fort for only three weeks, so perhaps the leitmotiv of the Manley family in times of stress was 'To Cornwall, to Cornwall'.[4]

At Salisbury she claims to have shared lodgings with the body of General Tollemache. Thomas Tollemache was wounded during the landing at Camaret Bay and brought back to Plymouth gangrened. He died on 12 June 1694 and on the Queen's orders the body was brought back to London to be interred at Westminster Abbey at royal expense. In fact, he was moved again from London and finally laid to rest at Helmingham in Suffolk. His monument is so large the church virtually had to be rebuilt around it.

Considering her apparent youth, Mrs Manley is quite precocious in her quotation-dropping – Horace, Cowley, Granville's translation of the choral ode from Seneca's Thyestes, *Plutarch's* Life of Themistocles *(which, it is apparent from this and other quotes, she read in Amyot's French translation) and Madame d'Aulnoy's* Memoirs of the Court of Spain.

This last work obviously made a great impression on the young Delarivier Manley for it is a model for her bestsellers, Secret Memoirs from ... the New Atalantis *and* Memoirs of Europe.

The author of Memoirs of the Court of Spain, *Marie Catherine de la Motte, Baronne d'Aulnoy, wrote three novels of contemporary gossip:* Mémoires de la cour d'Espagne *(1679–81),* Mémoires sur la cour de France *(1692) and* Mémoires de la cour d'Angleterre *(1695) and also the famous fairy tales,* Contes nouvelles ou les fées à la mode *(1698), a volume which includes 'The Blue Bird'. Born in the mid-seventeenth century she married François de la Motte, Baron d'Aulnoy in 1666. With her mother she instigated a prosecution for high treason against her husband. The conspiracy was exposed and the two women fled to England, and thence to Spain. Eventually in exchange for secret services to the French government they were allowed to return to France, where her writings about the high society she had encountered in exile titillated and entertained.*

The Diverting Works of the Countess d'Anois *were not printed in London until 1707 when Mrs Manley's popularity as a writer of secret memoirs was in the ascendant, and Mrs Manley's* A Lady's Paquet Broke Open *was published in two parts, bound with d'Aulnoy's* Memoirs of the Court of England *and* Memoirs of the Earl of Warwick.

1 Preface to 'A Stagecoach Journey to Exeter', 1725
2 Stanley J. Kunitz and Howard Haycroft, New York, 1952
3 *The Adventures of Rivella*, p. 85
4 Calendar of State Papers, Domestic series, 1680–1681, p. 400

5

A Female Wit

*Late in 1695 Mrs Manley returned to London with her first play, the work
of her two years' solitude. Soon after her return her letters written on the
stagecoach were anonymously published. She had them quickly withdrawn
claiming that it was not her desire to have them made public.*

*The path for women playwrights was already clear. Eighteen of Aphra
Behn's plays had already been presented, and Ariadne's* She Ventures
and He Wins *at Lincoln's Inn Fields Theatre in the autumn of 1695 led
the second wave of Restoration women playwrights.*

In December 1695 the Drury Lane production of Catherine Trotter's
Agnes de Castro *was greeted by a poem of support by Delarivier Manley.*

To the Author of *Agnes de Castro*

Orinda* and the fair Astrea† gone,
Not one was found to fill the vacant throne:
Aspiring man had quite regained the sway,
Again had taught us humbly to obey;
Till you (Nature's third start in favour of our kind)
With stronger arms their empire have disjoined,
And snatched a laurel which they thought their prize,
Thus, conqueror, with your wit, as with your eyes.
Fired by the bold example, I would try
To turn our sexes weaker destiny.
Oh, how I long, in the poetic race,

*Orinda: Katherine Phillips (1631–64), the first woman to have a play produced
by a professional London theatre company.
†*Astrea:* Aphra Behn, the first professional English woman playwright.

To loose the reins and give the glory chase;
For, thus encouraged and thus led by you,
Methinks we might more crowns than theirs subdue.

                                        Dela Manley

Soon afterwards, in the early spring of 1696, Mrs Manley's comedy, The
Lost Lover, *was performed, like* Agnes de Castro, *by the inferior of the
two professional London companies at Drury Lane Theatre. The cast included the young Colley Cibber.*

*Actor and dramatist, Cibber joined the Drury Lane Company in 1690.
His first comedy,* Love's Last Shift, *was performed in 1696. An unrepentant plagiarist, he regularly stole plots and speeches from other people's
plays. Also in the cast was Susannah Verbruggen, whom Cibber hailed as
'mistress of more variety of humour than I ever knew in any one woman
actress',[1] and the low comedian Joe Haines*

Song from The Lost Lover

To love and all its sweets adieu,
To glittering hopes and glowing fires,
To eyes that swore she would be true,
And yield Philander his desires.
Those dear, those faithless, perjured eyes,
Those fatal, sweet, deluding things;
The shepherd now forgiving dies,
And dying, mournfully, he sings:
Kinder death than cruel she,
Haste, oh haste to set me free.

*Mrs Manley was not happy with the actors, and the actors were not happy
with her. Given this miserable situation, it is impossible to judge whether
the play's failure was entirely due to the fact that it is not very good.*

PREFACE TO THE PRINTED EDITION OF THE LOST LOVER

This comedy, by the little success it met with in the acting, has
not at all deceived my expectations. I had ever so great a distrust
and so impartial an opinion that nothing but the flattery of my
friends (and them, one you'd imagine made of too much sense to
be so grossly mistaken, and without whose persuasion I never designed publishing of it) could in the last have held me in suspense
of its good or evil fortune, and to confess my fault, I own it an un-

pardonable one to expose, after two years' reflection, the follies of seven days (for barely in that time the play was wrought), and myself so great a stranger to the stage that I had lived buried in the country and in the six foregoing years had actually been but twice at the house.

The better half was cut. They say 'thas suffered by it, though they told me 'twas possible to have too much of a good thing, but I think never too little of an ill.

That knowledge I had of the Town was the genteel part, which does not always afford diverting characters. My design in writing was only to pass some tedious country hours, not imagining I should be so severely repaid. I now know my faults, and will promise to mend them by the surest way: not attempting to repeat them.

I am now convinced writing for the stage is no way proper for a woman, to whom all advantages but mere nature are refused. If we happen to have a genius to poetry it presently shoots to a fond desire of imitation. Though, to be lamely ridiculous, mine was indulged by my flatterers, who said nothing could come from me unentertaining. Like a hero not contented with applause from conquests, I find myself not only disappointed of my hopes of greater, but even to have lost all the glory of the former.

Had I confined my sense, as before, to some short song of Phillis, a tender billet, and the freedom of agreeable conversation I had still preserved the character of a witty woman.

Give me leave to thank the well-natured Town for damning me so suddenly. They would not suffer me to linger in suspense, nor allow me any degree of mortification. Neither my sex, dress, music and dancing could allow it a three days' reprieve, nor the modesty of the play itself prevail with the ladies to espouse it.

Here I should most justly reproach myself if I did not make all due acknowledgements for Sir Thomas Skipwith's civility. His native generosity and gallantry of temper took care nothing on his part should be wanting to make it pleasing.

Once more, my offended judges I am to appear before you, once more in possibility of giving you the like damning satisfaction. There is a tragedy of mine rehearsing, which 'tis too late to recall. I consent it meet with the same fortune. 'Twill forever rid me of a vanity too natural to our sex and make me say with the Grecian hero 'I had been lost if I had not been lost.'

They object the verses wrote by me before *Agnes de Castro*,

75

where, with poetic vanity, I seemed to think myself a champion for our sex. Some of my witty critics make a jest of my proving so favourable an enemy, but let me tell them this was not designed a consequence of that challenge, being writ two years before, and cannot have a smaller share in their esteem than mine.

After all, I think my treatment much severer than I deserved. I am satisfied the bare name of being a woman's play damned it beyond its own want of merit.

I will conclude with Dionysius, that Plato and philosophy have taught me to bear so great a loss, even of fame, with patience.

It is impossible to know whether Mrs Manley walked out on the Drury Lane actors in favour of the infinitely superior Lincoln's Inn Fields Company, or she was booted out by them for a mixture of youthful arrogance, temperamental behaviour and the unfair advantage of her influence over their master, Sir Thomas Skipwith (see Chapter 6 for a full account). Whichever, her tragedy, The Royal Mischief, *was performed, with an all-star cast including Thomas Betterton, Elizabeth Barry, Anne Bracegirdle, and Edward Kynaston, at Lincoln's Inn Fields Theatre in April 1696.*

Betterton was the greatest actor of the Restoration period, despite a low voice, small eyes and an ungainly figure. During the season before The Lost Lover *Betterton led an uprising of Drury Lane's leading players against their manager, Rich, and set up the rival company, with the actresses Mrs Barry and Mrs Bracegirdle at Lincoln's Inn Fields Theatre.*

Anne Bracegirdle was brought up by Betterton because her own father had a large brood of children, and she naturally turned to the stage for a career. Making her name as an ingénue, she was an excellent singer with a set of even, white teeth, and was much sought after for romantic leads. Desire for her drove men to madness. The actor, William Mountford (Susannah Verbruggen's husband), was murdered by Captain Hill in 1692 in a duel for her affection. Mrs Manley described her as one of 'the usefullest as well as the most agreeable women of the stage'.

Elizabeth Barry, the greatest tragic actress of the Restoration period, had a background similar to Mrs Manley. Daughter of an impoverished Cavalier, she was brought up by relatives and friends, and came into the theatre through the influence of her guardian, Sir William Davenant, the patent-holder of the Duke's Company. She was a protégée of Nell Gwyn and had affairs with some of the most attractive men of her generation including John Wilmot, Earl of Rochester, by whom she had a daughter. She was frequently the butt of scandal-sheets and satires, and often con-

ducted herself in a manner which encouraged gossip. She published a harrowing collection of love letters written to her by the playwright Thomas Otway, whom she had rejected, and she actually stabbed an actress during a performance of Lee's The Rival Queens *in a row over a veil. She gave English lessons to Mary of Modena who rewarded her with her wedding dress and coronation robes to wear as costumes.*

Edward Kynaston made his name as a boy who specialized in women's roles (before the introduction of actresses) with the King's Company. Described by Pepys as 'the prettiest woman in the whole house',[2] he was in part responsible for the decline in opposition to the women's début. No moralist could possibly argue that his habit of riding out to the park dressed in skirts and petticoats (his costumes), hotly pursued by his female fans, was preferable to letting women on the stage.

The Royal Mischief *was a* succès de scandale.

EXCERPT FROM THE ROYAL MISCHIEF

(The beautiful, but married, Princess Homais (Mrs Barry) is led into the chamber by her ex-lover, Ismael. Acmat, her eunuch confidant, awaits her with the handsome Prince Levan Dadian, her husband's nephew, also married. It is their first meeting, and it is love at first sight. It may be awful verse, but it is wonderful theatre.)

ISMAEL *leads* HOMAIS *in*

LEVAN: By heav'n, a greater miracle than heav'n can show.
 Not the bright empress of the sky
 Can boast such majesty. No artist could
 Define such beauty. See how the dazzling
 Form gives on; she cuts the yielding air, and
 Fills the space with glory. Respect should carry
 Me to her, but admiration here has
 Fixed my feet, unable to remove.

HOMAIS: Where shall I turn my guilty eyes?
 Oh, I could call on mountains now to sink my shame,
 Or hide me in the clefts of untried rocks,
 Where roaring billows should outbeat remembrance.
 Love, which gave courage till the trial came,
 That led me on to this extravagance,
 Proves much more coward than the heart he fills,
 And, like false friends in this extremity,

Thrusts me all naked on to meet a foe
Whose sight I have not courage to abide.

(*She leans on* ISMAEL *and holds her handkerchief to her face*)

LEVAN: Permit me to take this envious cloud away
That I may gaze on all the wonders there.
Oh, do not close those beauteous eyes, unless
Indeed you think there's nothing here deserves
Their shining.

HOMIAS: The light in yours eclipses mine.
See how they wink and cannot bear your lustre.
Oh, could I blush my shame away, then I
Would say your charms outgo my wishes
And I'm undone by too much excellence.

LEVAN: As strangers a salute is due. Were the
Protector here, he'd not refuse it.

(*They kiss*)

'Tis ecstasy and more. What have I done?
Her heart beats at her lips, and mine flies up
To meet it. See the roses fade, her swimming
Eyes give lessening light, and now they dart no more.
She faints! By heav'n, I've caught the poison
Too, and grow unable to support her.

(*She sinks down in a chair, he falls at her feet*)

ACMAT: He's caught, as sure as we live.
Her eyes have truer magic than a philtre.
We'll not intrude into a monarch's secrets.
The god of love himself is painted blind,
To teach all other eyes they should be veiled
Upon his sacred mysteries.

(*He shuts the scene, screens and curtains are drawn to conceal the couple.*)

Not surprisingly scenes of such unbridled lust coming from the pen of a young woman led to a few raised eyebrows and by the time the play was printed, Mrs Manley was again on the defensive.

PREFACE TO THE PRINTED EDITION OF
THE ROYAL MISCHIEF

I should not have given myself and the Town the trouble of a preface if the aspersions of my enemies had not made it necessary.

I am sorry those of my own sex are influenced by them and receive any character of a play upon trust without distinguishing ill-nature, envy and detraction in the representor.

The principal objection made against this tragedy is the warmth of it, as they are pleased to call it. In all writings of this kind some particular passion is described. As a woman, I thought it policy to begin with the softest, and which is easiest to our sex; ambition &c. were too bold for the first flight. All would have condemned me if, venturing on another, I had failed, when gentle love stood ready to afford an easy victory. I did not believe it possible to pursue him too far, or that my laurel should seem less graceful for having made an entire conquest.

Leonora* in *The Double Discovery* and part of *Aureng-Zebe*† have touches as full of natural fire as possible. I am amazed to know the boxes can be crowded and the ladies sit attentively and unconcerned at the Widow Lackitt and her son Daniel's‡ dialect, yet pretend to be shocked at the meaning of blank verse, for the words can give no offence.

The shutting of the scene I judged modester, as being done by a creature of the princess, than in any terms to have had both the lovers agree before the audience and then retire, as resolving to perform articles.

The pen should know no distinction. I should think it but an indifferent commendation to have it said she writes like a woman.

I am sorry to say there was a princess more wicked than Homais. Sir John Chardin's *Travels to Persia*, whence I took the story, can inform the reader that I have done her no injustice unless it were in punishing her at the last, which the historian is silent in.

Bassima's§ severer virtue should incline my audience to bestow

Leonora: from Dryden's *The Spanish Friar; or the Double Discovery.*
†*Aureng-Zebe:* by John Dryden.
‡*Widow Lackitt and her son Daniel:* from Thomas Southerne's *Oroonoko.*
§*Bassima*: the virtuous wife of Prince Levan Dadian.

the same commendation which they refuse me for her rival's contrary character.

I do not doubt when the ladies have given themselves the trouble of reading and comparing it with others they'll find the prejudice against our sex, and not refuse me the satisfaction of entertaining them, nor themselves the pleasure of Mrs Barry, who, by all that saw her, is concluded to have exceeded that perfection which before she was justly thought to have arrived at. My obligations to her were the greater since, against her own approbation she excelled and made the part of an ill-woman not only entertaining but admirable.

Unfortunately the Drury Lane company was not impressed by Mrs Manley's new-found notoriety, but, rather, decided to cash in on it with the anonymous satire The Female Wits, *a devastating attack on Mrs Manley, her tragedy, and her two sister-playwrights, the fat Mary Pix who wrote cracking comedies and turgid tragedies, and Catherine Trotter, a pious bluestocking. It also contains some savage digs at the rival players, in particular Betterton, Barry and Bracegirdle.*

Eight of the actors who had appeared in The Lost Lover *were proud enough of the content of* The Female Wits *to appear as themselves. One of them was George Powell, giving a ruthless impersonation of Betterton.*

The leading role, Marsilia (Mrs Manley), was taken by Susannah Verbruggen, who had been rejected by the Lincoln's Inn Fields Company, and Colley Cibber (who aspired to more power than even the incomparable Barry/Betterton/Bracegirdle trio held at this time) played Marsilia's idiot friend Praiseall. The first scene of The Female Wits *is set in the poetess Marsilia's dressing room.*

THE FEMALE WITS (ANONYMOUS) 1696–7
Act One, Scene One

A dressing room. Table and toilet furnished.
Enter MARSILIA (**Mrs Manley**) *in a night gown, followed by* PATIENCE (*her maid*).

MARSILIA: *Why, thou thoughtless, inconsiderable animal! Thou drivelling, dreaming lump! Is it not past nine o'clock? Must not I be at the rehearsal by ten, Brainless? And here's a toilet scarce half furnished!*

PATIENCE: *I am about it, madam.*

MARSILIA: *Yes, like a snail! 'Mount, my aspiring spirit! Mount! Hit yon azure roof, and justle gods!'* (Repeats).

PATIENCE: *Madam, your things are ready.*

MARSILIA: *Abominable! Intolerable! Past enduring!* (Stamps) *Speak to me whilst I am repeating! Interrupting wretch! What a thought more worth than worlds of thee! What a thought I have lost! Ay, ay, 'tis gone beyond the clouds.* (Cries) *Whither now, mischievous? Do I use to dress without attendance? So, finely prepared, Mrs Negligence! I never wear any patches!*

PATIENCE: *Madam?*

MARSILIA: *I ask you if ever you saw me wear any patches? Whose coo-maid wert thou, prithee? The barbarous noise of thy heels is enough to put the melody of the muses out of one's head. Almond milk for my hands. Sour! By heaven this monster designs to poison me.*

PATIENCE: *Indeed, madam 'tis but just made. I would not offer such an affront to those charming hands for all the world.*

MARSILIA: *Commended by thee! I shall grow sick of 'em. Well, but Patty, are you not vain enough to hope from the fragments of my discourse you may pick up a play? Come, be diligent, it might pass amongst a crowd, and do as well as some of its predecessors.*

PATIENCE: *(Nothing but flattery brings my lady into a good humour.) With your ladyship's directions I might aim at something.*

MARSILIA: *My necklace.*

PATIENCE: *Here's a neck! Such a shape! Such a skin!* (Trying it on) *Oh, if I were a man, I should run mad!*

MARSILIA: *(Humph! The girl has more sense than I imagined. She finds out those perfections all the Beau Monde have admired.) Well, Patty, after my third day I'll give you this gown and petticoat.*

PATIENCE: *Your ladyship will make one of velvet, I suppose.*

MARSILIA: *I guess I may. See who knocks.*

(PATIENCE goes out and returns.)

PATIENCE: *Madam, 'tis Mrs Wellfed.*

MARSILIA: *That ill-bred, ill-shaped creature! Let her come up. She's foolish and open-hearted. I shall pick something out of her that may do her mischief, or serve me to laugh at.*

PATIENCE: *Madam, you invited her to the rehearsal this morning.*

MARSILIA: *What if I did? She might have attended me at the Playhouse. Go, fetch her up.*

(Enter MRS WELLFED (Mrs Pix) and PATIENCE.)

WELLFED: *Good morrow, madam.*

MARSILIA: *Your servant, dear Mrs Wellfed, I have been longing for you this half hour.*

WELLFED: *'Tis near ten.*

MARSILIA: *Ay, my impertinence is such a trifle. But, madam, are we not to expect some more of your works?*

WELLFED: *Yes. I am playing the fool again. The story is . . .*

MARSILIA: *Nay, for a story, madam, you must give me leave to say, there's none like mine. The turns are so surprising, the love so passionate, the lines so strong, 'gad I'm afraid there's not a female actress in England can reach 'em.*

WELLFED: *My language!*

MARSILIA: *Now you talk of language, what do you think a Lord said to me t'other day? That he had heard I was a traveller, and he believed my voyage had been to the poet's Elyzium, for mortal fires could never inspire such words! Was not this fine?*

WELLFED: *Extravagantly fine! But, as I was saying . . .*

MARSILIA: *Mark but these two lines.*

WELLFED: *Madam, I have heard 'em already. You know you repeated every word of your play last night.*

MARSILIA: *I hope, Mrs Wellfed, the lines will bear being heard twice and twice, else 'twould be bad for the sparks who are never absent from the Playhouse, and must hear 'em seventeen or eighteen nights together.*

WELLFED: *How, madam! That's three or four more than* The Old Bachelor* *held out.*

MARSILIA: *Madam, I dare affirm there's not two such lines in the play you names. Madam, I'm sorry I am forced to tell you, interruption is the rudest thing in the world.*

WELLFED: *I am dumb. Pray proceed.*

MARSILIA: *Pray observe:*
> *'My scorching raptures make a boy of Jove;*
> *That ramping god shall learn of me to love.*
> *My scorching . . .'*

WELLFED: *Won't the ladies think some of those expressions indecent?*

MARSILIA: *Interrupting again, by heav'n! Sure, madam, I understand the ladies better than you. To my knowledge they love words that have warmth and fire etcetera in 'em. Here, Patty, give me a glass of sherry, my spirits are gone. No, manchet sot! Ah! The glass not clean! (She takes this opportunity because she knows I never fret before company.) I! Do I use to drink a thimble-full at a time?* (She throws it in her face.) *Take that to wash your face.*

PATIENCE: *(These are poetical ladies with a pox to 'em.)*

MARSILIA: *My service to you, madam, I think you drink in a morning.*

WELLFED: *Yes, else I had never come to this bigness, madam, to the increasing that inexhausted spring of poetry that it may swell, o'erflow, and bless the barren land.*

MARSILIA: *Incomparable, I protest!*

PATIENCE: *Madam Calista to wait upon your ladyship.*

MARSILIA: *Do you know her, child?*

WELLFED: *No.*

MARSILIA: *Oh, 'tis the vainest, proudest, senseless thing. She pretends to grammar, writes in mood and figure, does everything methodically. Poor creature! She shows me her works first. I always commend 'em,*

---

*The Old Bachelor: a hit comedy by William Congreve.

with a design she should expose 'em, and the Town be so kind to laugh her out of her follies.

WELLFED: That's hard in a friend.

MARSILIA: But 'tis very usual. Dunce! Why do you let her stay so long?

(Exit PATIENCE. Re-enter with CALISTA (Mrs Trotter).)

My best Calista! the charming'st nympth of all Apollo's train, let me embrace thee!

WELLFED: (So, I suppose my reception was preceded like this.)

MARSILIA: Pray know this lady, she is a sister of ours.

CALISTA: (She's big enough to be the mother of the Muses.) Madam, your servant.

WELLFED: Madam, yours.

(They salute.)

MARSILIA: Now here's the female triumvirate. Methinks 'twould be but civil of the men to lay down their pens for one year and let us divert the town. But if we should, they'd certainly be ashamed ever to take 'em up again.

CALISTA: From yours we expect wonders.

MARSILIA: Has any celebrated poet of the age been lately to look over any of your scenes, madam?

CALISTA: Yes, yes, one that you know, and who makes that his pretence for daily visits.

MARSILIA: But I had rather see one dear player than all the poets in the kingdom.

CALISTA: Good gad! That you should be in love with an old man!

MARSILIA: He is so with me. And you'll grant 'tis a harder task to rekindle dying coals than set tinder on a blaze.

WELLFED: I guess the spark. But why then is your play at this house?

MARSILIA: I thought you had known 'thad been an opera, and such an opera! But I won't talk on't till you see it. Mrs Wellfed, is not your lodgings often filled with the cabals of poets and judges?

WELLFED: *Faith, madam, I'll not tell a lie for the matter, they never do me the honour.*

MARSILIA: (to CALISTA) *I thought so when I asked her.*

WELLFED: *My brats are forced to appear of my own raising.*

MARSILIA: *Nay, Mrs Wellfed, they don't come to others to assist, but admire.*

1 *An Apology for the Life of Colley Cibber*
2 'Diary', Samuel Pepys, 18 August 1660

6

The Dangerous Swain

THE ADVENTURES OF RIVELLA
pages 42–52

Sir Charles continues.

Behold another wrong step towards ruining Delarivier's character with the world: the incense that was daily offered her upon this occasion from the men of vogue and wit. Her apartment was daily crowded with them.

I had still so much concern for Delarivier that I pitied her conduct, which I saw must infallibly centre in her ruin. There was no language approached her ear but flattery and persuasion to delight and love. The casuists told her a woman of her wit had the privilege of the other sex since all things were pardonable to a lady who could so well give laws to others yet was not obliged to keep them herself.

Her vanity was now at the height, so was her gaiety and good humour, especially at meat. She understood good living and indulged herself in it. Delarivier never drank but at meals, but then it was no way lost upon her, for her wit was never so sparkling as when she was pleased with her wine.

I could not keep away from her house, yet was stark mad to see her delighted with every fop who flattered her vanity. I used to take the privilege of long acquaintance and esteem to correct her ill-taste and the wrong turn she gave her judgement in admitting adulation from such wretches as many of them were (though indeed several persons of very good sense allowed Delarivier's merit and afforded her the honour of their conversation and esteem). She looked upon all I said with an evil eye, believing there was still jealousy at the bottom. She did not think fit to correct a conduct which she called very innocent for me, whose passion she had never valued. I still preached and she still went on her own way without any regard to my doctrine till experience gave her enough of her indiscretion.

A certain gentleman who was a very great scholar and master of abundance of sense and judgement, at her own request, brought to her acquaintance one Sir Thomas Skipwith, intending to do her service as to her design of writing for the theatre, that person having then interest enough to introduce upon one stage whatever pieces he pleased.

This knight had a very good face but his body was grown fat. He was naturally short and, his legs being what they call somewhat bandy, he was advised to wear his clothes very long to help conceal that defect, insomuch that his dress made him look shorter than he was.

He was following a handsome lady in the Mall after a world of courtship and begging her in vain to let him know where she lived. Seeing she was prepared to leave the park, he renewed his efforts, offering to go down upon his knees to her to have her grant his request. The lady turned gravely upon him and told him she thought he had been upon his knees all this time. The knight, conscious of his duck legs and long coat, retired in the greatest confusion, notwithstanding his natural and acquired assurance.

Sir Thomas was supposed to be towards fifty when he became acquainted with Delarivier, and his constitution broken by those excesses of which in his youth he had been guilty. He was married young to a lady of worth and honour who had brought him a very large jointure. Never any woman better deserved the character of a good wife, being universally obliging to all her husband's humours. The great love she had for him, together with her own sweetness of temper, made him infinitely easy at home. But he was detestably vain and loved to be thought in the favour of the fair, which was indeed his only fault, for he had a great deal of wit and good nature. But, sure, no youth of twenty had so vast a foible for being admired. He wrote very pretty well-turned *billets-doux*. He was not at all sparing of his letters when he met a woman who had a knack that way.

Delarivier was much to his taste, so that presently there grew the greatest intimacy in the world between them. But because she was a woman of fire, more than perhaps he could answer, he was resolved to destroy any hopes she might have of a nearer correspondence than would conveniently suit with his present circumstances by telling her his heart was already prepossessed. This served him to a double purpose: first, to let her know that she was reciprocally admired and, secondly, that no great things were to be expected from a person who was engaged or rather devoted to another.

He made Delarivier an entire confidante of his amour, naming fine Mrs Pym, then of the City, at the head of her six tall daughters not half so beautiful as their mother. This affair had subsisted ten years according to the knight's own account. The lady had begun it herself (falling in love with him at the Temple revels*) by letters of admiration to him.

After some time, corresponding by amorous high-flown *billets*, she granted a meeting, but was three years before she would let him know who she was, though there were most liberties but that of the face allowed. Afterwards they met without any of that reserve. It cost the knight, according to his own report, three hundred pounds a year (besides two thousand pounds' worth of jewels presented at times) to see her but once a week and give her a supper. He managed this matter so much to his own vain false reputation that it was become a proverb amongst his friends: 'Oh, 'tis Friday night, you must not expect to see Sir Thomas!'

He put a relation of his own into a house and maintained her there only for the conveniency of meeting his mistress. This creature in some time proving very mercenary and the knight unwilling to be imposed upon, she dogged the lady home and found out who she was. When once she had got the secret she made Sir Thomas pay what price she pleased for her keeping it. Not that his vanity was at all displeased at the Town's knowing his good fortune, for he privately boasted himself of it to his friends, but this baggage threatened to send the husband and his own lady news of their amour.

Behold what a fine person Delarivier chose to fool away her reputation with. I am satisfied that she was provoked at the confi-

Temple revels: these were derived from a traditional Temple ritual in which a mock prince held court, but by the late seventeenth century the Temple revels were more like an annual society ball.

dence he put in her and thought herself piqued in honour and charms to take him away from his real mistress. She was continually bringing in the lady's age in excuse of which the knight often said Pym was one of those lasting beauties that would have lovers at fourscore. He often admired the delicacy of her taste, upon which Delarivier was ready to burst with spleen, because she would not permit her husband any favours after she was once engaged with his worship, her conduct and nice reasoning forcing the good plain man to be contented with separate beds.

Sir Thomas was, however, exactly scrupulous in doing justice to the lady's honour, protesting that himself had never had the last favour (though she loved him to distraction) for fear of consequences. Yet she never scrupled to oblige him so far as to undress and go even into the naked bed with him once every week, where they found a way to please themselves as well as they could.

Delarivier was wild at being always entertained with another woman's charms. Skipwith used to show her Mrs Pym's letters, which were generally as long as a tailor's bill, stuffed with the *faux brillant*, which yet fed the knight's vanity and almost intoxicated his brain. He had found an agreeable way of entertaining himself near Delarivier by talking incessantly of his mistress. He did not pass a day without visiting and showing her some of her *billets-doux*. Meantime he was so assiduous near Delarivier that Mrs Pym took the alarm. He always sat behind her in the box at the play, led her to her chair, walked with her in the park, introduced her to his lady's acquaintance and omitted no sort of opportunity to be ever in her company. Delarivier put on all her arts to engage him effectually, though she would never hear that she had any such design.

But what else could she mean by a song, which I am going to repeat to you, made upon the knight's dropping a letter in her chamber writ by his darling mistress, wherein she complained of his passion for Delarivier. It began thus: 'It is in vain you tell me that I am worshipped and adored when you do things so contrary to it.' Delarivier immediately sent it back to him enclosed with these verses.

> Ah, dangerous swain, tell, tell me no more
> Of the blest nymph you worship and adore;
> When thy filled eyes are sparkling at her name
> I, raving, wish that mine had caused the flame.

> If by your fire for her you can impart
> Diffusive heat to warm another's heart,
> Ah, dang'rous swain, what would the ruin be,
> Should you but once persuade you burn for me?

Though possibly this might be only one of the thoughtless sallies of Delarivier's wit and fire, yet it was of the last consequence to her reputation.

The knight was perfectly drunk with vanity and joy upon receiving such agreeable proofs of his merit. He caused the words to be set to notes, and then sung them himself in all companies where he came. His flatterers, who were numerous, and did not now want to learn his weak side, gave him the title of the dangerous swain, which he prided himself in till his mistress grew downright uneasy and would have him visit Delarivier no longer.

He capitulated, as reason good, and would be paid his price for breaking so tender a friendship and what so agreeably flattered his vanity, which in short was, as the scandalous chronicle speaks, that his mistress should go to bed with him without reserve.

Either the weakness of his constitution or the greatness of his passion was prejudicial to his health. He grew proud of the disorder and went into a course of physic, as if it were a worse matter, finding it extremely to his credit that the town should believe so well of him (for upon report of a fair young lady, whom he had brought to tread the stage, that he had passed three days and nights successively in bed with her without any consequence, he was thought rather dangerous to a woman's reputation than her virtue) he would smile and never disabuse his friends when they rallied him upon his disorder.

For some time poor Delarivier's character suffered as the person that had done him this injury till, seeing him equally assiduous and fond of her in all public places, joined to what the operator discovered of his pretended disease. The world found out the cheat, detesting his vanity and Delarivier's folly, that could suffer the conversation of a wretch so insignificant to her pleasures and yet so dangerous to her reputation.

This short-lived report did not do Delarivier any great prejudice amongst the crowd of those who followed and flattered her with pretended adoration. She would tell me that her heart was still untouched, bating a little concern from her pride to move old

Skipwith's, who so obstinately defended it for another. 'Tis true she often hazarded appearances by indulging her natural vanity, and still continued to do so, though perhaps with more innocency than discretion, till the person came who indeed fixed her heart.

THE FACTS

Sir Thomas Skipwith, second baronet of Methseringham, Lincolnshire, was born in 1652. Educated at Gray's Inn, he was brought into Parliament as MP for Malmesbury at a by-election in 1696 but is not known to have ever spoken, and is not named on any of the important committees. In addition he was King's Sergeant at Law, Captain in the 13th Foot, and Master Keeper of West Hainault Walk, Waltham Forest 1692–1701. His character can be well illuminated from the manner of his business dealings.

Although he had no working knowledge of the theatre, he had been a shareholder in the royal patent of the Drury Lane Theatre since 1687. In December 1693, Skipwith, with the parsimonious Christopher Rich, took control of the company. Within weeks they seriously offended Thomas Betterton, by giving all his best roles to the young George Powell, as well as both Anne Bracegirdle and her friend Elizabeth Barry by giving all Mrs Barry's best parts to Mrs Bracegirdle. Mrs Bracegirdle, honourably, declined the offer. By April 1695, Betterton and the other leading players had had enough of the Rich/Skipwith administration, and they set up a new company in the old Lincoln's Inn Theatre. The Drury Lane Company practically threw out serious drama in favour of buffoonery, rope and ladder dancing and tumbling. In 1697, Betterton petitioned against Skipwith, accusing him of debasing the theatre until he had 'almost levelled it with Bartholomew Fair'.[1] The Dorset Garden, a theatre on the river designed by Wren and with a prestigious tradition (which was also owned by Rich and Skipwith) was used for, amongst other things, a lottery and exhibitions of strength by the 'Kentish strong man'.

Ultimately unsatisfied with his financial turnover, Skipwith sold his share in the patent to his close friend, Colonel Henry Brett for 10 shillings. But when Brett's patent started to make money, Skipwith brought a suit in Chancery for the recovery of his share, alleging that the grant to Brett had only been in trust.

He was married to Margaret Brydges, daughter of George Brydges, sixth Baron Chandos, by whom he had two children, a son and a daughter. In his will dated 1705, however, he acknowledged that his wife kept a separate establishment. In a codicil dated ten days before his death in June 1710, he leaves £1000 to Susan Gurney, 'his present housekeeper', and her daughter Charlotte was constituted the heiress to some of Skipwith's Lincolnshire property. Presumably Susan Gurney was one of his acknowledged mistresses, and Charlotte their illegitimate daughter. Contemporary gossip, quite independent of Mrs Manley, suggested that he had mortgaged his house to his mistress.[2]

Mrs Manley's song to Skipwith, 'Ah dangerous swain', was sung in Act One, Scene One of her play, The Lost Lover. *The first two lines differ slightly*

> On, dangerous swain, tell me no more,
> Thy happy nymph you worship and adore;

Whether it was used first in the play or in her letter to Skipwith is impossible to determine.

1 Lord Chamberlain's papers 7/3. PRO
2 Transcript of article on Skipwith from *The History of Parliament Trust*

7

The Greatest Mistress of Nature

THE ADVENTURES OF RIVELLA
pages 52–53, 64–72, 101–108

Sir Charles Lovemore continues.

I am going to show you a gentleman of undoubted merit, accomplished both from without and within. His face was beautiful, so was his shape till he grew a little burly. He was bred to business, as being what you call in France, one of the long robe.

His natural parts prodigious, which were happily joined by a learned and liberal education. His taste delicate in respect of good authors, remarkable for the sweetness of his temper and, in short, every way qualified for being beloved wherever he should happen to love.

Valuing myself as I do upon the reputation of an impartial historian, neither blind to Delarivier's weaknesses and misfortunes, as being once her lover, nor angry and severe as remembering I could never be beloved, I have joined together the just and the tender, not expatiated with malice upon her faults, nor yet blindly overlooking them. If I have happened, by repeating her little vanities, to destroy those first inclinations you may have had to esteem what was valuable in her composition, remember how hard it is in youth, even for the stronger sex, to resist the sweet poison of flattery and well-directed praise or admiration . . .

At that time Delarivier lived in a pretty retirement some few miles out of Town, where she diverted herself chiefly with walking and reading.

One day Mrs Trotter, her sister authoress (with whose story I may hereafter entertain you, as well as with the other writing ladies of our age), came, as usual, to make her a visit. She told her that John Tilly, a friend of hers, one of the most accomplished persons living, was in custody of a sergeant of arms for some misdemeanours, which were nothing in themselves, but as he had been of council on Lord Montagu's side against Lord Bath and was supposed to have had the chief conduct of the last trial, matters were like to be partially carried, because John Manley (poor Delarivier's kinsman and husband, though she always hated his being called so) was appointed chairman of the committee ordered to examine Tilly, and John Manley being long known a champion for Lord Bath in respect of his cause, it was very justly feared that he would join revenge and retaliation to his own native temper of choler and fury, by which means Tilly was to expect a very severe usage, if not a worse misfortune.

To conclude, after Mrs Trotter had raised Delarivier's pity, wonder and curiosity for the merit, beauty and innocence of the gentleman under prosecution, she proposed a real advantage to herself if she could influence her kinsman to stand neuter in the cause, or if that was not to be expected, that she would so far engage him that he should keep away on the day which was appointed for Tilly's examination.

Delarivier was always inclined to assist the wretched. Neither did she believe it prudence to neglect her own interest when she found it meritorious to pursue it. She told Mrs Trotter that being only her friend was enough to engage her to endeavour at serving this Tilly, whoever he were, but that since she had taken care to add interest to friendship, which were motives her circumstances were no way qualified to refuse, she was resolved upon that double consideration, to attempt doing whatever was in her power for both their services. But because she was not willing to embark without some prospect of a fortunate voyage she desired to speak with Tilly in person, as well as to inform herself of the merits of the cause as to be acquainted with a gentleman of whom she had given so advantageous a description.

Mrs Trotter blushed at the proposal which, Delarivier observing, immediately asked her if he were her lover, which would be enough to engage her to serve him without any other motive, and thereupon said that she would be contented to take minutes from

Mrs Trotter only, without concerning herself any further about being acquainted with Tilly.

Mrs Trotter, who was the most of a prude in her outward professions and the least of it in her inward practice, unless you'll think it prudery to allow freedoms with the air of restraint, asked Delarivier with a scornful smile, what was it she meant? Tilly was a married man, and, as such, out of the capacity to engage her secret service. Her friendship was merely with his wife, and, as such, if she would assist him she should be obliged to her for her trouble.

Delarivier, who hates dissimulation, especially amongst her friends, was resolved to pique Mrs Trotter for her insincerity and therefore said since it was so she insisted upon seeing and informing herself with Tilly's own mouth, or else she would not engage in the business.

The next day Tilly sent a gentleman to wait upon Delarivier and beg her interest in his service, together with the promise and assurance of a certain sum of money if she should succeed.

These preliminaries settled, the day after, Tilly sent the same person, who happened to be a sort of an insignificant gentleman, acquainted long since both with Delarivier and himself, in a chariot with an unknown livery to bring her to town and even to the sergeant at arms' house where Tilly was at that time confined.

Delarivier had formed to herself what it was going to speak to a man of business in private, that she must at least wait till the crowd were dismissed and therefore took a book in her pocket that she might entertain herself with reading whilst she waited for audience. She chose the Duke de la Rochefoucauld's *Moral Reflections*.

She had not attended long before Tilly came to wait on her, though but for two or three moments till he could dismiss his company, praying her to be easy till he might have the honour to return.

During this short compliment Delarivier had thrown her book upon the table. Tilly, whilst he was speaking, took it up, as not heeding what he did, and departed the room with the book in his hand. Who that has ever dipped into those reflections does not know that there is not a line there but what excites your curiosity and is worth being eternally admired and remembered? Tilly had never met with it before. He formed an idea from that book of the genius of the lady who chose it for entertainment and, though he had but an indifferent opinion hitherto of woman's conversation, he believed Delarivier must have a good taste from the company she kept. He found an opportunity of confirming himself before he parted in Delarivier's sense and capacity for business, as well as pleasure, which were agreeably mingled at supper, none but those two gentlemen and Delarivier being present. Behold the beginning of a friendship which endured for several years, even to Tilly's death.

He was married young, but as yet knew not what it was to love. His studies and application to business, together with the desire of making himself great in the world, had employed all his hours. Neither did his youth and vigour stand in need of diversions to relieve his mind. He was civil to his lady, meant very well for her children and did not then dream there was anything in her person defective to his happiness that was in the power of any other of that sex to bestow. Early in the morning Delarivier went to Westminster Hall. She took up her post at the bookseller's shop by the foot of those stairs which go up to the Parliament House.

She had not waited long but she saw her kinsman. He was covered in blushes and confusion, not imagining what business she had there unless to expose him. He had not even seen her face in some years, nor she his, having sought nothing so much as to avoid one another.

Delarivier advanced to speak with him. He blushed more and more. Several members coming by to go to the House and observing him with a lady in his hand, he thought it was best to take her from that public place and therefore led her the back way out of the Hall, called a coach, put her in it and afterwards got in himself, without having power to ask her what business brought her to enquire after him in a place so improper for conversation, at the same time ordering the coachman out of town.

Thus was that important affair neglected. They chose another chairman for the committee which sat that morning. Tilly was acquitted with the usual reprimand and ordered to be set at liberty, very much to the regret of John Manley when he came coolly to consider how scandalously he had abandoned an affair of that importance and which Lord Bath had left to his management.

Before Delarivier parted with her spouse she told him what was her designed request and the motive. He seemed very well pleased that nothing but interest had engaged her. He bid her be sure to cultivate a friendship with Tilly, who would doubtless come to return his thanks for the service she had done him, recommending to her at the same time, first, not to receive the money which had been promised her, because there were better views and which would be of more importance to her fortune and, secondly, to leave her house in the country for some time to come and take lodgings in London where he would wait upon her to direct her in the management of some great affair.

Behold Delarivier in a new scene – that of business, in which, however, love took care to save all his own immunities. He bespoke the most considerable place for Tilly, who often visited her with a pleasure new and surprising to his hitherto insensible breast.

I was lately come to Town. Delarivier's conversation always made part of my pleasure, if not my happiness, so that whenever she allowed me that favour I never omitted waiting on her. Some presentiment told me this agreeable gentleman would certainly succeed. I saw his eyes always fixed on her with unspeakable delight whilst hers languished him some returns. He approved rather than applauded what she said, but would always shift places till he got one next her, omitting no opportunity to touch her hand when he could do it without any seeming design.

I told her she had made a conquest and one that she ought to value herself upon, for Tilly was undoubtedly a man of worth as well as beauty. She laughed and said he was so awkward and so unfashioned as to love, that if he did bear her any great goodwill she was sure he neither durst, nor knew how to tell it her.

I perceived the pleasure she took in speaking of him. Wherefore I came in with my old way of caution and advice bidding her have a care. One affair with a married man did a woman's reputation more harm than with six others. Wives were, with reason, so implacable, so envenomed against those who supplanted them that they never forbore to revenge themselves at the expense of their rival's credit, for, if nothing else ensued, a total deprivation of the world's esteem was sure to be the consequence of an injured wife's resentment.

Tilly was too handsome a man to be lost with any patience. His wife was much older than himself and much a termagant, therefore nothing but fire and fury could be expected from such a domestic evil, the deprivation of a charming husband's heart being capable to rouse the most insensible. Delarivier laughed and thanked me for my advice, but how she profited by it a very little time will show us...

During their mutual intelligence and friendship, Mrs Trotter, after a long disuse, came to visit Delarivier. Tilly was then in the room. They both looked so amazed and confounded that Delarivier took the first occasion to withdraw, to permit them an opportunity to recover their concern... When she had ended her visit, Delarivier would know what had occasioned their mutual confusion. He laughed and defended himself a long time, at length he confessed Mrs Trotter was the first lady that ever made him unfaithful to his wife.

Her mother being in misfortunes and indebted to him, she had offered her daughter security. He took it and moreover the blessing of one night's lodging, which he never paid her back again. Delarivier laughed in her turn because Mrs Trotter had given herself airs of not visiting Delarivier now she was made the town talk by her scandalous intrigue with Tilly.

Much about that time George, Prince of Hesse-Darmstadt* came the second time into England. He had been viceroy of Catalonia towards the latter end of Charles II's† reign.

The inclination his Highness had of returning into Spain, his adorations for the dowager, his relation being no secret, made him keep up his correspondence with the Catalans, principally with the inhabitants of Barcelona, who continually solicited him to aid them with force whereby they might be enabled to declare themselves against Philip of Bourbon, whom they unwillingly obeyed. The Prince of Hesse represented this to the Court of England as a matter of very great importance. He produced several letters from the chief persons of Catalonia.

His Highness was recommended to a merchant in the city, whom he prayed to introduce him into the acquaintance of some of the most ingenious ladies in the English nation. This merchant was acquainted with a gentlewoman that was newly set up to sell milliner's ware to the ladies and gentleman. She was well born and encouraged by several persons, who laid out their money with her

*George Hesse-Darmstadt: son of Ludwig, second Landgrave of Hesse-Darmstadt, from his second marriage, was one of the leading figures in the War of the Spanish Succession. He spent the summer of 1703 in England.

†Charles II: King of Spain, whose death in 1700 was the climax to the problem of the Spanish Succession.

in consideration of her misfortunes. The merchant desired she would speak to the lady Delarivier, who was her customer, and two ladies more to come one evening to cards at her house, where himself would introduce the Prince incog.

His Highness understood nothing of Loo* which was the game they played at. He could not speak a word of English, nor the other ladies a word of French. They knew his quality, though they were to take no notice of it and thought to win his money, which is all that most ladies care for at play.

Delarivier sat next the Prince and, for the honour of the English-women, would not let him be cheated. She assisted him in his game and, in conjunction with his good luck, ordered the matter so well that his Highness was the only person who rose a winner.

From that time he conceived the greatest esteem for Delarivier. The Prince presented her with his picture at length and continued a correspondence with her till the day before his death.

Tilly did not believe there was any mixture of love in it because it was well known the Prince had engaged his heart in Spain and his person in England, by way of amusement, to a certain celebrated lady who had made a great figure in Flanders and was more known by the name of the Electress of Bavaria than her own name.

Delarivier tasted some years the pleasure of retirement in the conversation of the person beloved. But a tedious and an unhappy law-suit straightened Tilly's circumstances and put him under several difficulties.

In the meantime his wife died. Delarivier was complimented upon her loss even by Tilly himself, for all the world thought he loved her so well as to marry her. She received his address with such confusion and regret that he knew not what to make of her disorder till at length, bursting forth into tears, she cried, 'I am undone from this moment! I have lost the only person who secured me the possession of your heart.'

Tilly was struck with her words. I came into the room and Delarivier withdrew to hide her concern. Tilly felt himself so wounded by what she had spoken that I shall never forget it. He confessed her to be the greatest mistress of nature that ever was born. She knew, he said, the hidden springs and defects of humankind. Self-love was indeed such an inherent evil in all the world that he was afraid Delarivier had spoken something that looked too like the

*Loo: a popular card game.

99

truth. But whatever happened he should never be acquainted with a woman of her worth, neither could anything but extreme necessity force him to abandon her innocence and tenderness.

Not long after, Tilly was cast at law, and condemned in a great sum to be paid by the next term.

He concealed his misfortunes from Delarivier but she learned them from other persons.

One must be a woman of an exalted soul to take the part she did. The troubles of the mind cast her into a fit of sickness. Tilly guessed at the cause and endeavoured to restore her at any price, having assured her of it. She asked him if he would marry her. He immediately answered he would, though he were ruined by it. She told him that was a very hard sentence, she could not consent to his ruin with half so much ease as her own, then enquired if there was any way to save him. He explained to her his circumstances and the proposals that had been made to him of courting a rich young widow, but that he could not think of it.

Delarivier paused a long time, at length, pulling up her spirits and fixing her resolution, she told him it should be so. He should not be undone for her sake. She had received many obligations from him, and he had suffered several inconveniences on her account... She was proud it was now in her power to repay part of the debt she owed. Therefore she conjured him to make his addresses to the lady, for though he might be so far influenced by his bride as afterwards to become ingrateful, she would much rather that should happen than to see him poor and miserable, an object of perpetual reproach to her heart and eyes, for having preferred the reparation of her own honour to the preservation of his.

I should move you too far ... in relating half that tenderness and reluctance with which it was concluded they should part. I was the confidant between them. But though I had esteem and friendship for Tilly there was something touched my soul more nearly for Delarivier's interest, therefore I would have dissuaded her from that romantic bravery of mind by advising her to marry her lover who was so bright a man that he could never prove long unhappy, his own capacity being sufficient to extricate him. But as she had never taken my advice in any thing, she did not begin now. There was a pleasure, she said, in becoming miserable when it was to make a person happy by whom she had been so very much obliged and so long and faithfully beloved.

Tilly's handsome person immediately made way to the widow's heart. It is not my business to speak much of her, though the theme be very ample. I have heard him say that he might have succeeded to his wish if he could have had the confidence to believe a woman could have been won so quickly. Her relations got notice of the courtship and represented the disadvantage of the match, which occasioned settlements and security of her own fortune to her use.

Tilly trusted to the power he hoped to gain over her heart, thinking when once they were married she might be brought to recede, but he was mistaken.

The wooing lasted but a month, with all the obstacles her friends could raise, which perhaps was a fortnight longer than the date of her passion afterwards.

Fears and jealousies ensued. They passed many uneasy hours of wedlock together. He teased the lady about cards and she him for Delarivier, who seldom saw him, for she led her life mostly in the country and never appeared in public after Tilly's marriage, which, with four years' uneasiness, concluded in the loss of his senses and, in three more, of his life. Whether the want of Delarivier's conversation, which he had so long been used to, contributed, or the uneasiness of his circumstances, for his marriage had not answered the fancied end, or something else which I am not willing to say where very much may be said (though as Delarivier's friend I have no reason to spare Tilly's lady, because she always speaks of her with language most unfit for a gentlewoman and on all occasions has used her with the spite and ill-nature of an enraged, jealous wife).

After that time I know nothing memorable of Delarivier but that she seemed to bury all thoughts of gallantry in Tilly's tomb and, unless she had herself published such melting scenes of love, I should, by her regularity and good behaviour, have thought she had lost the memory of that passion.

THE FACTS

John Tilly was always in trouble, yet he managed to keep up his law practice in the Inner Temple, and his position as Governor of the Prison at the Fleet – even when he was inside it as a prisoner.

In the House of Commons in 1696 a committee was set up to consider how the abuses of prisons and other privileged places might be regulated. Tilly was cited for releasing prisoners in exchange for cash: 20 or 30 guineas per person was the going rate. The actor Hudson, for example (who played Ismael in Mrs Manley's The Royal Mischief*), was appearing on stage when still technically a prisoner.*

In two years Tilly was said to have made £8000 in gratuities, chamber rents, commitment fees and other perquisites. In turn he also spent a fortune in bribes. Miss Ann Hancock, who appeared against him, had warned him against a man who was perjured. 'Tilly answered that he had occasion for such men; for that the rule of his prison extended to the East and West Indies and when any person was sued to an execution he could but look over the Bar and have two witnesses to swear he was then actually in prison, though he was forty miles off. She then asked Mr Tilly what would he do if this matter was brought into Parliament House? To which he said, what would you do there? For there I can do what I will withal, they were such a company of bribed villains . . . She then said if it was so she must go to the House of Lords: to which he replied it was only palming five or six talking lords with 100 guineas apiece and they would quash all the rest . . . and as for the judges they were all such a parcel of rogues that they would swallow his gold faster than he would give it to them.' The House was told how 'Tilly's money flew about like feathers out of an opened feather bed in a windy day.'[1]

John Manley, MP, was on the committee.

Amongst other charges against Tilly, a case was heard by the Lords in February 1697 in which he was ordered to pay '£500 down due on bond and £20 costs', and on 6 May 1701, the House of Lords committed Tilly to the custody of Black Rod for 'reflecting against their lordships'.[2]

The financial trouble he got into before leaving Mrs Manley to marry an heiress came on 2 March 1702 when the King's Bench Court ruled against Tilly and he was ordered to pay Thos. Richardson £1000.[3]

John Manley and John Tilly were also in conflict over the Albemarle case in which the Earl of Bath and Ralph, Earl of Montagu were in dispute over the disposition of the estate of the Duke of Albemarle. John Manley represented Lord Bath, Tilly, Lord Montagu.

The Montagu v. Bath case was one of the longest and most expensive suits of the century, a sort of seventeenth-century Jarndyce v. Jarndyce. The circumstances of the claimants were extraordinary, the spoils were incomes totalling £10,000 a year, and understandably the public followed avidly.

The second Duke of Albemarle wrote a will leaving his fortune to his cousin Lord Bath and the Granville family. It was backed up by a deed stating that it could not be revoked by any will not witnessed by, amongst others, three peers of the realm. He then wrote a new will – in Jamaica, where peers of the realm were in short supply, but where he was busily raising a sunken Spanish galleon and claiming its £40,000 treasure.

His wife, the main beneficiary of the second will, shortly went mad, and on her husband's death returned to England, declaring that she would marry only a reigning monarch.

With some initiative Ralph Montagu dressed himself as the Emperor of China and married the Duchess. Whilst her relatives tried to beat the door down he consummated the marriage, and from that moment vigorously championed his wife's claim through the Court of Chancery, the House of Lords and numerous appeals and counter-appeals. The case was still not fully settled when the Earl of Bath died in 1701.

The logic of such a case was that the lawyers would be the only people able to make a killing. John Manley certainly had plans of organizing things behind the scenes in order to make money for himself and his illegitimate son. However, despite its possibilities, the problem of the two lawyers having Delarivier Manley's friendship in common must have muddled their thinking for no one seems to have come out of it in pocket.[4]

Soon after the death of his first wife, Tilly married Margaret Smith, 26-year-old daughter of Sir John Reresby and widow of George Smith of Doctors Commons, on 12 December 1702. He died in 1705.[5]

Although Mrs Manley had welcomed Trotter's Agnes de Castro *with effusive verse, and the two had suffered under the satire of* The Female Wits, *Mrs Manley's opinion of her learned friend took a sharp nosedive.*

After some success with her first four plays, Mrs Trotter left London in 1701 and started to involve herself in religious and philosophical controversy. She returned in 1704 with a new play and probably infuriated Mrs Manley by writing a set of verses to the Duke of Marlborough on his victory at Blenheim. Shortly afterwards she abandoned Catholicism for the Church of England and set out to marry a clergyman, which she did in 1708. (He was the second one that had proposed.)

Mrs Manley was never fond of hypocrisy but these goings-on were not quite enough to merit the exposition Mrs Trotter was given in The New Atalantis. *Perhaps the gossip that Catherine Trotter had had an affair with John Churchill fuelled the fire, but presumably there is more than meets the eye in Mrs Manley's version of meeting Tilly through her learned friend to merit such scorn:*

NEW ATALANTIS II
page 266

The Earl of Halifax has a gallery adorned with the pictures of the ingenious, among which Mrs Trotter has the honour of a place. Whether seated there for her little talent in poetry or her larger one in amour I will leave to his lordship's decision.

NEW ATALANTIS II
pages 55–7

I could enumerate, were it not too tedious, many of Mrs Trotter's adventures, by which she was become the diversion of as many of the town as found her to their taste and would purchase. Yet she still assumed an air of virtue pretended and was ever eloquent, according to her stiff manner, upon the foible of others. She also fitted herself with an excellent mask called religion, having as often changed, and as often professed herself a votary to that shrine where was to be found the most apparent interest, or which priest had the greatest art of persuading... But a husband was Trotter's business: the only means to prevent her from falling, when her youth and charms were upon the wing, into extreme contempt.

Catherine Portmore, Countess of Dorchester, who had introduced her to the Cabal* but, with infinite anxiety, suffered that any lover should dare to engage where she had fixed her heart. But because narrow circumstances do not always suffer people to do what they would; Trotter was still forced to have lovers, though, if you'll believe her professions to her fair friend, they had no part in her inclination. In short, Lady Portmore, whose poetical genius did not much lead her to the better economy of her family, soon found the inconveniencies of it... Trotter's marriage crossed her delights. How does she exclaim against the breach of friend-

*Cabal: a group of society lesbians, including Elizabeth Dunch and her sister, Countess Falmouth, Lady Effingham, Lady Anna Frescheville, Lady Margaret Lexington, the opera singer Catherine Tofts, Queen Anne's attendant Mrs Proud, the Countess of Macclesfield, and John Churchill's daughter, Mary, Duchess of Montagu.

ship in the fair? How regret the authority of a husband who has boldly dared to carry his wife into the country where she now sets up for regularity and intends to be an ornament to that religion which she had once before abandoned and newly again professed? She will write no more for the stage – 'tis profane, indiscreet, unpardonable. Controversy engrosses all her hours. The muses must give place. If she have any fancy or judgement, we may justly expect to see something excellent from a hand so well fitted, if experience can fit, to paint the defects and beauties of those many opinions she has so often and so zealously embraced.

1 *The Journal of the House of Commons* XI, pp. 641–6; Tracts relating to Courts of conscience, prisons etc. British Library shelf-mark 816m15 (14) (16).
2 Luttrell, *Brief Relation*, IV, p. 181. Ibid, V, p. 46.
3 Calendar of State Papers, Domestic series, 1700–1702, p. 529.
4 E. F. Ward, *Christopher Monck, Duke of Albemarle*, 339–53; Dr Eveline Cruickshanks et al., Divisions in the House of Lords, *Bulletin of the Institute of Historical Research* LIII, 1980, pp. 75–6
5 J. Foster, *London Marriage Licences*, London, 1889, p. 1343

8

The Black Beau

During the desolate time which followed the loss of her lover, John Tilly, Mrs Manley's friend, Richard Steele, chose to snub her.

They had become friends at about the time of her theatrical début in 1696. Shortly afterwards, from 1697 to 1699, Steele, a soldier, was stationed on the Isle of Wight and during this time he wrote regularly to Mrs Manley. The letters (which deal mainly with love affairs and alchemy), printed in 1707 as part of The Lady's Paquet Broke Open, *and reissued in 1711 as part of* Court Intrigues, *anticipate in attitude the correspondence of Valmont and Merteuil in Laclos's* Les Liaisons dangereuses.*

COURT INTRIGUES
pages 62–73

Letter XV

... You never tell me any news.

I have none but love-toys; my mistress again flies me, but I will understand no other but that 'tis to be pursued, for I make love as I would lay a siege: 'tis not my business to consider whether I shall win the town or not, but I know it's my duty to lay my bones there or do it. I do not know what to talk to you longer, but know I can't end till the end of the paper. Let me hear how love thrives in Town, and also how you are now employed as to business.

Letter XVI

Madam,

The post is just going out, but the fellow waits for this to you, which he must never go without. Pray let me hear how the fire burns, and what's become of your sooty sage who you once seemed to listen to ... Are it and — again friends? Or has he that place mortgaged to him, or how? I am sure you are never out of an intrigue and I take it ill that I live in ignorance. I tell you all I am doing, which is following a wild, regardless, pretty innocent, that is a very woman, a natural artless tyrant.

There is an old gentlewoman in these parts, rich enough, would I believe have more pity on me and sees, though in spectacles, a broad back; but there's so much nitre and sulphur in the mine and that I can't think of digging there. The poor old lover attempts fifteen at me, and I swear I am sometimes in the humour of deserting her that's frozen in youth to take her that's warm in old age. The good lady is hallow, but not false; the girl's flippant but not kind. I am divided between horror and desire and tremble with both.

What will become of me? If this cruel fair goes on she will be the death of me, throw me into my grave, the matron, and bury my live coals in her ashes.

Letter XVII

It is an hour since I writ my last to you, and two since I heard from you ... I see you, madam, I see Venus as busy in the coals as ever Vulcan was, and riches affixed at last to a beauteous form and engaging mien.

I wish, madam, the charms of your person as immortal as those of your wit.

Letter XVIII

Madam,

... There is in no poet extant so perfect a description of a true wood-nymph as my mistress. I must despatch two or three clumsy rivals, besides a large attendant mastiff that always follows her, before my access is easy. She has an excellent wild beauty and wit, and everything that nature only can bestow.

I beseech you, if you see the hag (who is a perfect nightmare to my dreams) not to tell her you have heard from me.

Be pleased to write to me, for that fair hand can impart nothing but joy to . . .

Letter XIX

Madam,

You certainly believe me in love with you, or you would answer my letters. I know it my fate to be shunned when it comes to that.

We had yesterday a funeral here where my fair one was a bearer and I led one of the mourners. In the performance of that office 'twas no small diversion to the ill-natured company to observe her scuttle toward the grave to avoid poor me. But I assure her I'll follow her to it or my own, but we will lie in the same bed . . .

What's become of Mrs —? Does she still talk as loud as she talked of —? Give her my service, but let none know where I am.

Letter XX

Madam,

My having been a day or two out of this Island prevented the receipt of yours till today, wherein you give me the exalted station of lying at your feet. Believe hereafter the call for letters to be my passing-bell if you neglect writing. I cannot blame you, though I hate those that interrupt you, for who would not engross you? . . .

Pray tell me seriously whether you are perfectly assured in your secret. I can depend upon what you approve, for, though you have a great deal of wit, there's no deceiving you.

Letter XXI

Dear sir,

I give you this trouble to desire you'd do me the favour of a line or two that I may not look upon myself quite out of your thoughts when you come to an ευρεκα. My implicit faith deserves some consideration, and, when the philosophic world is to be disposed of, I hope there will some corner or other in it fall to my share.

If you have any account of the most renowned Mr W —, you'd

extremely oblige me to let me have it, for I am passionately taken
with his exemplary sincerity, who gave me a note of £100 and sent
me word I should never have it. I wish I could learn whether he
has been in Town of late, or not.

If you'll answer this impertinent paper you'll do an action suit-
able to your good nature and usual friendship to, Sir, . . .

Letter XXII

Madam,

Yours of the first was no small satisfaction to me, for I could not
imagine the reason of your silence. But I am glad to find you have
been in the country for I hope when I have next the happiness of
seeing you to be entertained with the effects of your leisure. 'Twas
impossible for that fair, elegant hand of yours to be unemployed
when you were in the seat of the muses, and rivers, hills, foun-
tains and fields were the charming objects of your imagination.

Letter XXIII

Madam,

. . . I cannot forbear talking to you all my soul, for you must be my
counsellor as well as you have been my protectress in several acci-
dents. I cannot forbear having hopes in your chymistry . . . There
is nothing so acceptable to me as to read from you, no, not the
pleasure of talking to you, which I must leave off lest I never enjoy
the other, as a just judgement on the impertinence of, madam,

Your most happy slave.

*She was his friend, confidante, mentor and adviser. During her affair with
Tilly, Steele was a frequent guest. Then, in 1702, when Tilly left her, she
asked Steele to lend her some money towards her fare into the country,
where she hoped to visit friends and recover her spirits. He refused her,
and, in so doing, threw the first handful in what was to become one of the
most bitter literary mud-slinging contests of the eighteenth century. It
raged through the pages of the* Examiner, *the* Guardian, Tatler *and Mrs
Manley's novels* New Atalantis, Rivella *and her political pamphlets
including 'The Honour and Prerogative . . .'.*

Mrs Manley, in the disguise of 'an airy wife', married to, and pregnant by, her gentleman husband, John Tilly, features in the tale of Monsieur L'Ingrat, alias Richard Steele, and the alchemist.

(Whether or not Mrs Manley was actually pregnant by Tilly is not known, but no child appears to have been born to the couple.)

NEW ATALANTIS I
pages 187–93

Oh, let me ease my spleen! I shall burst with laughter.

These are preposterous times for vice. D'ye see that black beau, stuck up in a pert chariot, thick-set, his eyes lost in his head, hanging eyebrows, broad face and tallow complexion? I long to inform myself if it be his own, he cannot yet, sure, pretend to that.

He's called Monsieur L'Ingrat. He shapes his manners to his name and is exquisitely so in all he does; has an inexhaustible fund of dissimulation and does not bely the country he was born in, which is famed for falsehood and insincerity; has a world of wit and genteel repartee. He's a poet too, and was very favourably received by the town, especially in his first performance, where, if you'll take my opinion, he exhausted most of his stock, for what he has since produced seem but faint copies of that agreeable original, though he's a most incorrect writer.

He pleases in spite of the faults we see and own. Whether application might not burnish the defect or if those very defects were brightened, whether the genuine spirit would not fly off, are queries not so easily resolved.

I remember him almost t'other day, but a wretched common trooper. He had the luck to write a small poem and dedicates it to a person whom he never saw, a lord that's since dead, who had a sparkling genius, much of humanity, loved the muses and was a very good soldier. He encouraged his performance, took him into his family and gave him a standard in his regiment.

The genteel company that he was let into, assisted by his own genius, wiped off the rust of education. He began to polish his manners, to refine his conversation and, in short, to fit himself for something better than what he had been used. His morals were loose. His principles nothing but pretence and a firm resolution of making his fortune at what rate soever. But because he was far from being at ease that way, he covered all by a most profound dissimulation, not in his practice but in his words; not in his actions but in his pen, where he affected to be extremely religious at the same time when he had two different creatures lying-in of base children by him.

The person who had done so much for him, not doing more, he thought all that he had done for him was below his desert.

He wanted to rise faster than he did.

There was a person who pretended to the great work, and he was so vain as to believe the illiterate fellow could produce the philosopher's stone and would give it him.

The quack found him a bubble to his mind; one that had wit and was sanguine enough to cheat himself and save him abundance of words and trouble in the pursuit.

Well! A house is taken and furnished, and furnaces built and to work they go. The young soldier's little ready money immediately flies off. His credit is next staked, which soon likewise vanishes into smoke.

The operator tells him 'twas not from such small sums as those he must expect perfection, what he had had hitherto was insignificant, or minute, as one grain of sand compared to the sea-shore, in value of what he might assure himself of in the noble pursuit of nature, that he would carry him to wait upon a gentleman very ingenious, who had spent more than ten times that sum in the hands of the ignorant, yet, convinced of the foundation, was ready to join with him for the expense to go on with a new attempt.

Accordingly, Monsieur is introduced to one, who was indeed a friend to the quack, but did not absolutely confide in his skill, though he still believed there was such a thing as the philosopher's stone. Yet, hearing how illiterate this pretended operator was, he could not imagine he had attained that secret in nature, which was never yet purchased at all but with great charge and experience.

This gentleman [Tilly] had an airy wife, who pretended to be a sort of a director in the laws of poetry, believed herself to be a very good judge of the excellencies and defects of writing.

She was mightily taken with Monsieur's conversation, prayed him often to favour her that way, being informed of the narrowness of his circumstances, she gave him credit to her midwife, for assistance to one of his damsels that had sworn an unborn child to him. The woman was maintained till her lying-in was over and the infant taken off his hands *par la sage femme* for such and such considerations upon paper. He had no money to give, that was beforehand evaporated into smoke.

Still the furnaces burnt on. His credit was stretched to the utmost. Demands came quick upon him and became clamorous. He had neglected his lord's business and even left his house to give himself up to the vian pursuits of chymistry.

The lady who had taken friendship for him [Mrs Manley] upon the score of his wit, made it her business to inform herself from her husband of the probability of their success. He gave her but cold comfort in the case, and even went so far as to tell her he believed that fellow knew nothing of the matter, though there was a great City hall taken and furnaces ordered to be built, that they might have room enough to transmute abundantly.

The operator had persuaded the young chymist to sell his commission, which he was very busy about, and even repined that he met not a purchaser as soon as he desired, for he thought every hour's delay kept him from his imaginary kingdom.

But it was to be feared when he had put the money into the doctor's hands to be laid out in mercury and other drugs that were to be transmuted into sol, as small a sum as it was, he would give him the slip and go out of the nation with it.

The lady was good-natured and detected the cheat. She begged her husband that he would give her leave to discover it. He advised her against it. It might do 'em both a mischief. But she insisted so much upon it that he bid her to do what she would.

The lady was then in childbed, among a merry up-sitting of the gossips. Monsieur made one his genius, sparkled amongst the ladies, he made love to 'em all in their turn, whispered soft thing to this, ogled t'other, kissed the hand of that, went upon his knees to a fourth, and so infinitely pleased 'em that they all cried he was the life of the company.

The sick lady was gone to repose herself upon the bed, and sent for Monsieur to come to her alone, for she had something to say to him.

Vain of his merit, he did not doubt but she was going to make him a passionate declaration of love, and how sensible she was of his charms. He even fancied she withdrew because possibly she was uneasy at those professions of gallantry he had been making to others.

He approached the bedside with all the softness and submission in his air and eyes, all the tenderness he well knew how to assume. The lady desired him to take a chair and afford her an uninterrupted audience in what she was going to say.

This confirmed him in his opinion, and he was even weighing with himself whether he should be kind or cruel, for the lady was no beauty, but lay all languishing in the becoming dress of a woman in her circumstances.

She entertained him very differently from what he expected. In short, she discovered the cheat and advised him to take care of himself and to withdraw from that labyrinth he was involved in as well as he could. He was undone if he sold his commission. All the world would laugh him to scorn and he would hardly find a friend to help him to another.

A thunderbolt falling at the foot of a frightful traveller could not more have confounded him than this did our chymist.

What! All his furnaces blown up in a moment? All evaporated into smoke and air? He could not believe it. The plumes, all elate and haughty as he appeared before, sunk upon his crest. Who would have believed there could have been such a shrinking of the soul? Such a contractedness of genius? Such a poorness of spirit? So abject a fall from so towering height? He was not able in half an hour's time to speak one word. His address was departed. He knew not what to say, only begged leave to retire.

'Twas necessary that he must go through the chamber where the ladies were to go to the stairs. He pulled his hat over his eyes, without seeing 'em, and away he went.

The lady was satisfied with doing the friendly and honest part, let him receive it how he would. The coquets fell upon her with violence, and asked her what she had done to Monsieur, what had she said to him that certainly bewitched him. Never was such an alteration for they had easily seen his change of countenance and air. She defended herself as well as she could and they were forced to conclude the entertainment without him.

The young chymist was so base (as he afterwards told the lady) to believe this only an artifice of her husband to keep the learned doctor to himself and deprive him of his share of philosophical riches. In this thought he mortally hated the discoverer. But his eyes being opened and his sight cleared he quickly saw the fallacy as plain as the sun at noon. He was already undone or very near it.

They had contracted abundance of debts. The doctor was a sort of an insolvent person. The creditors knew that and did not trouble their heads about him.

Steele was forced to abscond. All he could preserve from the chymical shipwreck was his commission.

This lady engaged her husband to serve him in his troubles and sent him perpetual advices when anything was like to happen to him. She prevented him several times from being persecuted by the implacable midwife.

He used to term her his guardian angel and everything that was generous and human.

But fortune did more for him in his adversity than would have lain in her way in prosperity. She threw him to seek for refuge in a house where was a lady with very large possessions. He married her. She settled all upon him and died soon after.

He remarried to an heiress who will be very considerable after her mother's decease, has got a place in the government and now, as you see, sparks it in Hyde Park.

The lady who had served him lost her husband and fell into a great deal of trouble. After she had long suffered she attempted his gratitude by the demand of a small favour, which he gave her assurances of serving her in. The demand was not above ten pieces to carry her from all the troubles to a safe sanctuary, to her friends a considerable distance in the country. They were willing to receive her if she came, but not to furnish her with money for the journey.

He kept her a long time, more than a year, in suspense, and then refused her in two lines by pretence of incapacity. Nay, refused a second time to oblige her with but two pieces upon an extra-ordinary exigency to help her out of some new trouble she was involved with.

It is not only to her, but to all that have ever served him he has showed himself so ungrateful. The very midwife was forced to sue him. In short, he pays nor obliges nobody but when he can't help it.

THE FACTS

Richard Steele was born in Dublin in 1672 and educated at Charterhouse and Oxford. John, Lord Cutts took Steele into his household as a secretary and procured for him a captaincy in Lord Lucas's Regiment of Foot. While still a soldier he wrote The Christian Hero *(1701), and followed this with three comedies for the stage.*

When he had girlfriend trouble Mrs Manley put Steele in touch with Mrs Phipps, the implacable midwife of Watling Street at the sign of the Coffin and Cradle.

His first wife was Margaret Stretch, née Ford, a widow, whom he married in the spring of 1705. She died in December 1706, leaving him £850 from her estates in Barbados. His second wife was Mary Scurlock, the 'dear Prue' of his letters, whom he married in August 1707. He is reported to have lived in considerable state after this marriage.

In April 1709, with Joseph Addison, he started the Tatler *and later the* Spectator.

Mrs Manley's indictment of Steele was published in May 1709. Early in September a letter from a 'Tobiah Greenhat', whom Mrs Manley assumed to be the editor himself, appeared in the Tatler *(No. 63):*

... The writer of 'Memoirs from the Mediterranean', who, by the help of some artificial poisons conveyed by smells, has within these few weeks brought many persons of both sexes to an untimely fate; and, what is more surprising, has, contrary to her profession, with the same odours, revived others who had long since drowned in the whirlpools of Lethe.

Also in September 1709 Steele wrote to Mrs Manley: 'I had not money when you did me the favour to ask a loan of a trifling sum of me. I had the greatest sense imaginable of the kind notice you gave me when I was going on my ruin.'

The following month Mrs Manley brought out the second volume of The New Atalantis, *and, in the dedicatory letter, has a stab at the* Tatler, 'who, though he allows ingratitude, avarice and those other vices which the law does not reach, to be the business of satire; yet, in another place he says, these are his words "that where crimes are enormous, the delinquent deserves little pity, but the reporter less". At this rate vice may stalk at noon secure from reproach.'

In May 1710 Mrs Manley dedicated her Memoirs of Europe *to Bickerstaff, Steele's byline in the* Tatler, *as he had called a patron the 'filthiest creature in the street', and therefore deserved to be one.*

September 1710 had Steele fighting back (Tatler, No. 229), claiming he had been: 'scolded at by a Female Tatler, and slandered by another of the same character under the title of Atalantis.

'I have been annotated, retattled, examined and condoled; but, it being my standing maxim never to speak ill of the dead, I shall let these authors rest in peace, and take great pleasure in thinking that I have sometimes been the means of their getting a belly-full.'

On 12 May 1713, following a constant stream of unfavourable comment in the Examiner (which had been edited by Jonathan Swift and Delarivier Manley) Steele wrote (Guardian LIII):

Others who have rallied me upon the sins of my youth tell me it is credibly reported that I have formerly lain with the Examiner . . . It is nothing to me whether the Examiner writes against me in the character of an estranged friend or an exasperated mistress.

Unfortunately for Steele, Swift and Mrs Manley had passed the Examiner over to Oldisworth. Swift wrote in Mrs Manley's defence, threatening Steele with his 'temper' and his 'style', and the new Examiner explained (Examiner, 22 May 1713) that he was now entirely responsible for the Examiner and asked for a reparation for offended innocence, reminding Steele 'that it ill became him amidst his penitential qualms to treat a great lady, in high favour with the Queen, in so slighting and indecent a manner'.

Flip, and unrepentant, Steele replied in Guardian LXIII:

I declare then it was a false report which was spread concerning me and a lady sometimes reputed author of the Examiner, and I can now make her no reparation but in begging her pardon, that I never lay with her.

I speak all this only in regard to the Examiner's offended innocence, and will make no reply as to what relates merely to myself.

Mrs Manley, not a woman to take an affront of this kind lying down, tossed a few more insults in Steele's direction with 'The Honour and Prerogative of the Queen's Majesty Vindicated and Defended against the unexampled insolences of the author of the Guardian, in a letter from a country Whig to Mr Steele' (1713) and 'A Modest Enquiry into the Reasons of the Joy expressed by a Certain Sett of People upon the spreading of a report of her Majesty's Death' (1714). Mrs Manley's literary venom was almost as much to do with politics as with her own grievances with Steele, and their political differences – Steele was a Whig, Manley a Tory – were heightened by the serious illness of Queen Anne, which put the whole country on tenterhooks.

Following publication of her (auto)biography, The Adventures of Rivella, *in 1714, which contains a few more snide remarks at Steele's expense, the whole situation seems to have cooled, and in 1717 the breach was publicly repaired.*

Steele, by now manager of the Drury Lane Theatre, bought Mrs Manley's play, Lucius, The First Christian King of Britain, *for 600 guineas. Accordingly, Mrs Manley dedicated the play to him.*

To Sir Richard Steele

When old men cast their eyes upon epistles of this kind, from the name of the person who makes the address, and of him who receives it, they usually have reason to expect applauses improper either to be given, or accepted, by the parties concerned.

I fear it will be much more so in this address than any other which has at any time appeared. But, while common dedications are stuffed with painful panegyrics, the plain and honest business of this is only to do an act of justice, and to end a former misunderstanding between the author and him whom she here makes her patron.

In consideration that one knows not how far what we have said of each other may affect our character in the world, I take it for an act of honour to declare, on my part, that I have not known a greater mortification than when I have reflected upon the severities which have flowed from a pen which is now, you see, disposed as much to celebrate and commend you. On your part, your sincere endeavour to promote the reputation and success of this tragedy are infallible testimonies of the candour and friendship you retain for me.

I rejoice in this public retribution, and with pleasure acknowledge that I find, by experience, that some useful notices which I had the good fortune to give you for your conduct in former life, with some hazard to myself, were not to be blotted out of your memory by any hardships that followed them.

I know you so well that I am assured you already think I have on this subject said too much; and I am confident you believe of me that I did not conceal much more. I should not say so much.

Be then the very memory of disagreeable things forgotten forever and give me leave to thank you for your kindness to this play, and, in return, to show towards your merit the same good-will.

But, when my heart is full and my pen ready to express the kindest sentiments to your advantage, I reflect upon what I have formerly heard you say: that the fame of a gentleman, like the credit of a merchant, must flow from his own intrinsic value, and that all means to enlarge it which do not arise naturally from that real worth, instead of promoting the character of either, did but lessen and render it suspicious.

I leave you therefore to the great opportunities which are daily in your power, of bestowing on yourself what nobody else can give you, and wishing you health and prosperity.

I omit to dwell upon some very late actions of yours in public, which unhappy prejudices had as little expected from you as the zeal and solicitude which you showed for my private interests in the success of this play.

I shall say no more, trusting to the gallantry of your temper for further proofs of friendship, and allowing you, like a true woman, all the good qualities in the world now I am pleased with you, as well as I gave you all the ill ones when I was angry with you.

I remain, with the greatest truth,

Sir,

your most humble,
most faithful, and
most obliged servant

De la Rivier Manley

She had, by keeping the compliments as ambiguous as possible, protected herself from any possible change of heart by Steele, who wrote a special prologue for the printed version of the play.

Prologue by Sir Richard Steele

Nat Lee, for buskins famed, would often say
To stage-success he had a certain way;
Something for all the people must be done,
And with some circumstance each order won.
This he thought easy, as to make a treat,
And for a tragedy gave this receipt:
Take me, said he, a princess young and fair,
Then take a blooming victor flushed with war.
Let him not owe to vain report renown,
But in the ladies' sight cut squadrons down;

Let him, whom they themselves saw win the field,
Him to whose sword they saw whole armies yield,
Approach the heroine with dread surprise,
And own no valour proof against bright eyes.
The boxes are your own – the thing is hit,
And ladies, as they near each other sit,
Cry 'Oh! How movingly the scene is writ!'
For all the rest, with ease delights you'll shape.
Write for the heroes in the pit a rape.
Give the first gallery a ghost. Oh th'upper
Bestow, though at that distance, a good supper.
Thus all their fancies, working their own way,
They're pleased and think they owe it to the play.
But the ambitious author of these scenes
With now low arts to court your favour means;
With her success and disappointment move
On the just laws of Empire and of love!

9

A Bristol Intrigue

Without Steele's financial assistance, Mrs Manley finally made her way to the west of England.

From Bristol she writes to a friend, 'Clorinda', about her slow recovery from the break-up of her affair with Tilly, and her subsequent exploits.

These letters were published in The Lady's Paquet Broke Open *which is a collection of letters, some of which are pure fact, others pure fiction, and some combining the two. The two parts were later reprinted under the title* Court Intrigues.

COURT INTRIGUES
pages 171–99

Yes, my dear, my ever valued friend, you shall know all that my poor tortured soul has suffered in these long, cruel three years' separation. Have I one spark of joy remaining in my soul, your letter brought it forth and, though dead to hope and lost to happiness, or even wish of happiness, I find still a pleasure in being esteemed by you.

Oh, Clorinda, in other loves there is no constancy, even friendship to me is but insipid, fit only to amuse a soul unfeeling a more exalted heat. Had our sex been different I fear, my dear, by this we had forgot to love, or perhaps have learnt to hate, though that's a passion so foreign to my mind that, as yet, I am ignorant of what it means. My soul rebounds not at an injury, engrossed by softer passions, it has no room to entertain so rough a guest.

You ask me the meaning of that melancholy strain that runs through all my letters and conjure me to explain myself with friendship. You will remember me that when we parted I was envied by most and by all thought happy. 'Tis true I had not suffered shipwreck then, but since. Oh, what I have not endured! Will you have patience to hear a three years' anguish? 'Tis all dark, a melancholy gloom. My gayer genius is fled and lost in its shades. I'm the reverse of what I was. No more the pleasure of the world, the delight of conversation, no more beloved, yet still loving. Is there a misery beyond this? Is there a rack in nature I have not felt? May I not well complain?

But, to give you in particular my misfortunes, you left me in the possession of a heart worthy mine, but the world and interest divided us. An eminent law-suit ruined my lover's fortune, in which part of mine was involved, and left him no hopes of repairing it but by a wife more rich than I could be. The coming term was to make him in execution for a sum too mighty for him to struggle with. This was kept a secret from me for fear of my disquiets.

At length, finding him excessively melancholy and dejected beyond what I could ever have suspected from his fortitude of soul, he told me his misfortunes, that he was undone. But his own sorrows were inconsiderable to him in comparison of mine. He was indeed by promise, by vows and inclination my husband. But, should I call him to the performance, we both were lost and must expect to languish out the rest of his life in prison oppressed with misery and wants.

That such a lady had been offered him for a wife, considerable in her fortune and so destitute of charms that it could not give me the least suspicion that inconstancy had any part in what was his only refuge, the last plank that could preserve me from shipwreck.

I took time to weigh and examine the truth of what he said, but was soon convinced of his ill circumstances and could not suffer my heart to hesitate a moment on what it should do to save him. The thoughts were death to me that for my sake he should live poor, contemned and wretched. I concluded that, though, like other men, he might prove ungrateful, 'twas a more tolerable evil than having him, through my means, unfortunate. Let all who have got generous souls, as I suppose they will, condemn me for what they may call weakness, but sure Clorinda does better know how to value so unprecedented a sacrifice.

I gave up all my happiness to his interest and by permission saw him three weeks after married. Indeed misfortunes in prospect are only guessed at, they are not to be described till felt. Though I had prepared myself for all that could be expected of sufferings, yet, when once I began to feel the real load, I sunk under 'em. Since he was safe and happy no matter what became of me, neither honour nor policy would permit his visits, for his engagements with me had been no secret. His lady would soon have heard of 'em and consequently have had her own and his pleasure poisoned that way.

Besides, I was resolved to put an end to a flame that could not now burn with innocence.

I gave myself up to the diversions of the world: visits, cards, plays, all that ought to divert the mind. My love was to suffer a violent death since it would not resign to a natural. But in vain it withstood the efforts of reason, diversions, duty. It mocked all my endeavours and, augmenting by resistance, threw me into a violent illness, out of which I did not, but after much danger, recover. The pain was at my heart, which the physicians had no cure for.

Then it was, my Clorinda, that with the rest of the world, you heard the report of my death, and truly I was so near it that it was the work of ten months before I could stand alone, or under my own hand give you to know I was not yet so happy as to be nothing.

They removed me into the country to try their last experiment, the change of air. By the time of my return back to London, almost two years had passed since that fatal marriage. My heart still engaged, still tortured by a love which I could not persuade myself to be criminal, because I once had a right and title to his love, though, when I considered myself had released all pretences, I doubly blamed my heart for persevering. But love is power too mighty for us to control.

I saw my murderer and my old wounds bled afresh at the fatal sight. He complained of his own want of happiness and secretly pleased my heart by finding, if his grief were less, his satisfaction was not more. How significant a relief is this? How is it that a power as mighty as love can be served and find its account in trifles? He complained that marriage had not answered his end, for, though it saved him from impending ruin in his law-suit and discharged his execution, yet, many other of his debts being unpaid, gave him much uneasiness; that his lady, like a right widow, had secured the greatest part of her fortune to her own use; their humours were extremely different and he had little hopes of prevailing on hers, because he wanted the first principles that should give his their agreeable motion; she loved flattery, as most ladies do, and he was not master of it (he had almost said of kindness too). In short, he was too dangerous for my conversation. His eyes had still the same beauty, his words their usual softness, and I think a certain melancholy air heightened all his charms.

Should I dwell on every circumstance the conversation must tire you. In a word, I tore myself from these enchantments and forbid my heart such criminal delights. Yet my torment pursued me wheresoever I fled.

I had once more recourse to the country and went, by recommendation, to board in Bristol at a gentleman's house, who, with his family, were all strangers to me.

A chronic distemper which my melancholy had contracted could only expect its cure from change of air.

The family I was received into consisted of an old well-natured gentleman, governed by his splenetic wife, who had as much cunning as nature alone could give her and, had her education been good, her wit might have been more considerable. They had formerly merchandized but, being pretty easy in the world, had lately left off. A brother of hers lived in the family, who had been bred up with them in their way. He appeared to me as a person well-made and handsome, but perfectly unfashioned, having had no conversation but business, who declined women's company and rarely ever spoke among the men. He seldom ate at home and I believe I was near seven months in the house with him before we had any conversation, though you know me easy of access, and pleased with company. My business was to seek diversion which my ill-health had made perfectly necessary to me. An ugly unmarried maid of thirty, a sister of theirs, brought up the rear of this goodly family and here, in reading and conversing with some of the town who visited Mrs Wouldbe, which you must know is my landlady's name, I passed a considerable time.

The poison still at my heart, daily wasting by a consuming hopeless fire, what would I not have done for my cure?

How was I, alone of all humankind, plagued with a never-dying passion? I had read, indeed, that inconstancy was counted the greatest weakness of the weakest sex, but here I imagined it would have been meritorious, for there can be no appeal from marriage. That certainly ought to destroy all precedent inclinations and they must be unpardonable who preserve theirs after it.

At length, another brother, the squire of Mrs Wouldbe's family, came upon a visit to Bristol. He dressed at the ladies, had seen some of the world, was half bred as to gallantry and about that pitch in understanding, but good-natured and a very honest gentleman. What his brother wanted in tongue, he supplied and 'twas not his fault if conversation languished. His kind endeavours would relieve it, though sometimes at the expense of his reputation as to wit (for 'tis very hard for great talkers always to escape impertinence).

Mr Peregrine Worthy was his name. He quickly told me that his heart had been mortgaged above these two years to a young lady passionately fond of him. But he was one whom her father would not permit her to marry because his estate did not answer the fortune he could give her. He was not so young as his brother by six years, nor so well shaped, but much more polished, and it came into my head, by a malicious diversion, to make him in love with me, notwithstanding his engagement. It seemed intolerable that any other woman should be a quiet possessor of the heart she loved whilst I was so unhappy to be deprived of what I had adored.

The general ill-omen of all man's constancy made me conclude I should have no great trouble in conquering Peregrine's. I looked not at the consequence, nor had debated with myself what to do with that toy, his heart, or that lumber, his person, were they once made an offering to me. What I wanted was present amusement, for, as poisons are said to expel poisons, I would with all my heart have loved anything to put out of my mind the phantom that haunted me.

But this was not the diamond that was to cut mine, for, though we entered into a commerce of gallantry and, after his departure, writ letters as mutually tender as if we had been really touched, I suppose we both remained unwounded by each other. All I know of my side is that my former passion found not the least abatement and therefore 'tis easy to conclude a new one did not succeed.

At length young Worthy fell so ill that his life was for some time in danger. Mrs Wouldbe had business called her to London. After she was gone I debated with myself whether I should be so ill-natured to let a brother of the family where I was die and never give him a visit. I knew he did not love company and, least of all, ladies', but my good manners and good nature over-ruling, I resolved to do my duty, though it should prove unacceptable.

I came to his bedside and had a much civiler reception than I expected. The height of his distemper, as I then supposed, had mastered his native roughness. I found him in a violent fever and, having too lately had an expensive experience of what physicians could do, I was able to advise him in many things proper for the recovery of his health. Had Mrs Wouldbe been there I should not have attempted it, for she has that quality peculiar to herself to believe none besides herself knowing in anything, and that she is ignorant of nothing.

Mrs Abigail, the surly, her sister, of thirty, dull and heavy in make as well as understanding, was his chief nurse. I had compassion for him in the ill hands he was in and therefore failed not to be often with him, which he seemed to receive very civilly.

His fever abated but, his temper being melancholy, the distemper had so seized his spirits that I found it must be a powerful diversion of the mind that could be able to throw it thence, but whence it should proceed I could not guess to a man wholly free from vice or passions. I found his understanding very good, what he did speak proper and well imagined and I doubted not but he would show us he had wit enough, could he once dispense with custom and modesty that had hitherto kept him silent.

We read to him books of wit and gallantry. I found he had a true taste of things and could commend in the right place. Thus a sort of satisfaction succeeded compassion and I felt myself better pleased in his company than I imagined I could have been. We grew acquainted. His conversation became free and genteel.

We chanced to talk of love. He protested he never new what the least spark of it meant and my judgement was he never would, not considering that nature makes nothing in vain. However, a defect of constitution might happen.

I talked of the language of the eyes. He innocently protested he knew not what I meant by that, neither could he imagine; nay, was more and more confounded when I told him lovers' eyes could talk. He assured me he never minded the differences of glances, he thought all eyes had the same looks, though not the same colour. This was wonderful, I thought, from one who had himself the finest I ever saw, and a very bad encouragement for me if I had had the least design upon his heart, though in jest, as before with his brother.

He liked my company, or my library, or both, so well that after he was up and dressed he never was from us. I suited him with the gay part of reading, being properest to remove his melancholy.

We chanced one day to light upon Brown's translation of Fontanelle's and Aristaenetus' letters.

He seemed mightily pleased with 'em. There was one from a lady who permits a lover all but the last favour and gives him leave to touch her breast, to kiss her eyes, her mouth and squeeze her with her stays off. He could not imagine what pleasure could be taken in that.

Not long after, we were returning, with Mistress Abigail, late from a visit out of town, where we had been merrily entertained and had all three, contrary to custom, drank enough to elevate us. Bacchus is counted a friend to love. After putting me into the coach, young Worthy stayed not for compliments with Mrs Abigail, but threw himself, with a gaiety wholly new to him, on the seat by me. 'Twas dark. Though the surly maid was our opposite, in the humour we were all in, it passed for raillery. He pretended to make the lady's experiment of squeezing, since he found I had only a morning-waistcoat on. Thence he attempted to kiss my cheek, then my lips, and, if I'm not mistaken, could no longer wonder where the pleasure was of that. After we came home we continued the frolic, sitting upon Mrs Abigail's bed. He sighed after every kiss, no ill-omen of a heart touched with pleasure.

I may truly protest to you that, for nine successive years that I had been tormented with an unintermitting passion, this was the only moment that I first found it suspended. I confess I was then lost to any thoughts but the present. There his eyes first gave, and knew the distinction of, looks. He could no longer boast of ignorance. They had a softness wholly new, so full of sparkling fire, so tender, nay, so passionate, that I catched the distemper into mine and looked on his with an uncommon pleasure. You may perhaps too nicely blame me for giving in to those delights, but I was suddenly betrayed by one from whom I never expected any danger and therefore could not arm myself against it.

I was also charmed with thinking myself the first that gave him wishes that gave him desire and joy. That heart, that formerly

insensitive heart, seemed no longer so to me. I was pleased to en-
courage a pleasure that destroyed my former pain and I found
young Worthy had, in an hour, done more towards my cure than
all my own whole two years' endeavours.

Mrs Abigail thought our conversation something too tender.
The wine working out in ill-nature with her, as in kindness with
us, she was impertinent enough to have offended us had she been
worth it. After this, when he found me alone, he would sometimes
pretend to the pleasure of a kiss, but never declared himself, so
that I believed myself mistaken when I reckoned upon my
conquest.

He took occasion always to be with me. We read. We walked.
We ate together. But still not a word of love.

He became unimaginably improved, like Cymon for Iphigenia
in the fable. [*John Dryden's* Fable.]

He dressed. He discoursed. He no longer avoided the ladies'
company. All the world wondered at the change. He became as
genteel as anybody and appeared with as good an air. I told you at
first that he was perfectly well-shaped. To me they attributed these
improvements, calling him my scholar.

My pain was inverted from London to the country. I would have
given all the world to hear his mouth confirm what his eyes had so
often told me.

What laws, what manners, what customs have our sex? How
must we be tantalized? How tortured? Why was it not permitted to
search his heart? Why not to ask him if yet he knew whether there
was a deity called love? Our perpetual opportunities, our long converse, might have well excused it. But modesty overruled even
curiosity and vanity. I was forced to suffer in uncertainty and
silence.

Thus a whole year run on since that moment he first began to
make an impression on my heart. At length, amidst the pleasing
liberty of unnumbered kisses, he brought out, with doubting
modesty, that transporting word 'I love you.' I could have swore
that till that minute I never knew what joy, what pleasure, was. I
could not stay for reflection. I could not speak.

I more than spoke. I hugged him in an ecstatic manner, more
charming, more intelligible than a thousand words.

You have known, my dear Clorinda, the force of love. Wonder
not then that thus, in me, he exerted his tyrannic sway, or think

the person I've described, because lower than myself in rank, unworthy of my heart. His was, by inclination, noble and Dryden, who so well knew the passions, tell us,

> Love either finds equality or makes it.
> Like death he knows no diff'rence in degrees,
> But plains and levels all.

After that he would perhaps have no longer scrupled to speak his passion, but our opportunities of being alone were so few. What was now no secret to me was long since, by his actions, suspected by the family.

Mrs Wouldbe and Mrs Abigail were our perpetual companions, nay, we had an additional spy, a friend of Mrs Wouldbe's that was received there upon some misfortunes of her husband. This was a damsel that pretended to airs and charms, would ogle my lover and, whether by their desires or her own inclinations, attempted to have made a diversion of his kindness. She offered at so many advances that my jealous eyes called 'em unpardonable. However her charms were no way dangerous and I believe I need have given myself no pain that way. This creature won upon my easy nature by her assiduities and she used often to rally at Mrs Wouldbe's fears for her brother.

Thus we were interrupted in the full course of our amour and 'twas impossible to speak without being overheard. One or both of the sisters were perpetually upon the hearken.

It was not so when any other company was with me, for I had a ridiculous pretender or two out of the town, which, had not my heart been engaged, might perhaps served me to laugh at. But I was ever uneasy, as well as Worthy, out of each other's company and, though we could only steal a glance or sometimes the touch of the hand, fancy improved our pleasures and made them greater than any other satisfaction out of ourselves. My first fires were in their full force, the object only changed by an invisible transmutation. I loved to the height of all my formed disorder, but it was with a more pleasing pain, a secret satisfaction, I having made a conquest over that hitherto inexorable virgin heart.

I conceive their fears were least young Worthy should marry me. I was a widow with an encumbered jointure and his affairs required a wife with a fortune in ready money. However, our intelligence had proceeded no further than the word love and it seems to me that he had not formed, no more than myself, any designs towards the possession of what he loved.

Mrs Wouldbe and Mrs Marwould (the name of the other lady) were invited to an entertainment in the town that was like to hold till late. Mrs Abigail was diverted another way, so that I was left alone, the old husband being abroad upon his occasions. Young Worthy, ignorant of their designs, for they kept it from us, was likewise from home.

The weather was hot. I undressed myself to a loose night-gown and Marseilles* petticoat and laid me down after dinner upon the bed to sleep.

Young Worthy returned by instinct, or the whispers of his good genius, as he calls it, and, hearing all were gone out, came as usual to my chamber. I cast my eyes to the door as it opened and saw him with so elevated a joy that scarce gave him time to shut it after him, for, running to me as I lay, he threw himself upon my mouth and eyes and so transportedly kissed me that I could no longer doubt but his modesty was giving place to his desires.

When, hearing somebody come up the stairs, which answered directly to my chamber, I broke from his arms and, opening the door, was ready to swoon at the sight of Mrs Wouldbe, returned very ill, or pretendedly so. She would have gone in but I shut it after me and directed her into the dining room.

She asked me who I had with me. I told her, in utmost confusion, a gentleman. She said, 'Why don't you then, madam, go to him?'

'So I must,' answered I and, returning, shut the door to after me, but the key was left on the outside.

Young Worthy saw my disorder and the guilty air which yet I could not recover. I told him, though we were never so innocent, all appearances were against us. My undress, the dishabille of the bed, the door shut upon us and my refusal to let her enter. So that, happen what would, for his sake, I was resolved his sister should not see him, who most diligently kept sentry in the dining room to watch who should come out.

I ran the hazard and scandal of being suspected with any rather than being confirmed with him.

She goes down to the servants to enquire who was with me. They tell her none but her brother, who was come in two moments before her. She returned again to her post in the dining room.

* Marseilles: a kind of stiff, ribbed cotton.

Having not so far lost her respect to attempt my chamber door though, as I told you, the key was on the outside.

I was at my wits' end for my invention and would have him get out of my dressing-room window upon the leads that answered to a window in another part of the house and which, by chance, was then open, from whence he might descend the back stairs and possibly get off unseen. He objected some men that were working in the next neighbour's yard. I told him in a case like that something must be hazarded and therefore, removing with expedition the glass and toilet that was spread upon a table under that window, he shot in a moment from one to the other and, good fortune favouring him, got down the stairs and through the house without any of their people seeing him. This was a lucky conveyance, successful legerdemain, and I, recovered from my fright, could not choose but laugh at the sick lady upon duty. She stirred not from her post (I wonder how her patience could hold from interrupting us?) till after three hours.

I calling for candles, she asked the servant who brought 'em who was with me and she, answering 'nobody', you must imagine what she could think! She had set one sentry at the street door, which, how they escaped seeing Worthy go out I can't imagine. Herself had been upon the watch above. I had told her there was a gentleman in the chamber with me; one maid says 'tis her brother and, soon after, another tells her there was nobody there; my apparent confusion and dishabille – all these were what confounded even her cunning. I believe till that minute she suspected not that her brother had discovered to me his love, but the appearances were now strong and she imagined us to be really criminal. Why should I of a sudden be so undressed? Why shut up alone with her brother, where she was refused entrance? Why so confused? These were indeed circumstantial evidences.

But what could I have said had she entered and found us as at first? It would certainly have condemned us and getting him off so was all that was left for us to do as making the best of a bad market.

'Twas at worst a moot point whether he was with me or no. Politic Mrs Wouldbe said nothing to her brother or me, but kept close, as well as Abigail, to their watch. We had not time to speak together for above a week after.

One night he put a paper into my hand, which I have transcribed because your curiosity may be obliged by reading a first love letter, without art or ornament, the effects only of what that passion could dictate, for it seemed to me 'twas to get the better of his modesty that could not, had we had opportunity, so freely permit him to explain himself.

THE FIRST LETTER
(expressing the desire of a young lover under constraint)

Tell me, my dear, inspiring mistress, how shall I express the tender passion of my love? Instruct your willing scholar and give directions by what means I may obtain an uncontrolled access to your dear person without the apprehension of dispiriting fear. The geniuses that haunt your chamber prevent the pleasure of your private conversation and puts me into insupportable pain to suppress the appearance of the glowing flames of love raging in my breast.

If you would preserve my life, you must suddenly find out some way how, uninterrupted, I may freely taste the sweets of love. 'Tis not in the power of human nature unproved to conceive the inestimable pleasures of powerful love, a pleasure so great and so transporting that 'tis inexpressible.

My thoughts too eagerly press upon another and strive which shall tell you first how much I love. To describe your bright charms is too great an attempt for my weak genius. I dare only say I feel the effect in ecstasy and rapture. I doubt not but your goodness will excuse and pardon all defects of nature, especially when you've my heart a sacrifice for all.

Oh, inconstancy! But why that thought? What needs have I to fear? Have not I received marks of special favour? But 'tis a woman! Yet the best of her sex, all truth and goodness. Ay, but human nature, in all things, love changes. The highest tides produce the lowest ebbs.

Remember fair one, who taught me first to love, who brought me into this labyrinth. Will you now desert me? Will you now leave me to be lost inevitably? Tell me truly. Or, if I'm lost, tell me and at all I'm past recovery, 'tis not in the power of time, the coolest thoughts of reason, nothing less than death can unfix my love, grounded upon so firm an esteem, riveted immovable within my heart. I faint. Give me life. Let me live and live to love you.

To tell you the pleasure this letter gave me would too much confirm you in the opinion of my weakness. The next day, being Sunday, Mrs Marwould went with me to church and, as I was kneeling, I could not forbear taking out the paper to read it. I thought her at her devotions and never minded her squint over my shoulders. Whence she gained the first part of the letter, which confirmed her opinion, from the sight of the character whence it came.

My lover, for a night or two after, stayed in my chamber later by half an hour than the rest. The door was open and we could not speak so low but we were overheard. Those precious moments, those delightful embraces, those piercing kisses never to be recalled! All was at the mercy of Mrs Wouldbe, who, by hearkening, gave herself a confirmation to her fears and, the second night, met him at his own chamber door, as he came from me, with millions of reproaches. I knew nothing of what was passed till, the next night, he put this second letter into my hand.

THE SECOND LETTER
(excusing himself from being any more alone)

'Tis impossible to express the concern with which I write to you upon this unpleasant subject. We were overheard, if not seen, last night by my married sister. She received me at the head of the stairs, shut my chamber door and began to open.

I was not so much surprised as I thought I should have been upon such an occasion. She said she could not believe what she had been told, had not her own ears convinced her as to the truth of it. She recounted to me many particular passages, especially that when you, in so much confusion, thrust her out of the room when you had only a night-gown on and I in the chamber with you.

I answered that she has given herself a great deal of trouble to little purpose, I did not suppose but she'd a truer opinion of both, that indeed I liked to be with you because you were improving and delightful company, but no farther, and that a jealous listener, hearing imperfectly some words and not others, turned all to the subject they were apprehensive of, or suspected, if the talk was never so remote, nothing more uncertain when the sound of words cannot be distinguished. I urged my own innocence.

So we parted and appeased her pretty well upon the promise never to be alone with you again, since it gave her so much uneasiness.

Lest you should be ignorant of what has passed, I thought it proper this way to acquaint you with it, that you might not judge untruly of my neglect. The hazard is at present too great for me to break my promise, therefore, if you have, and I can't think otherwise, a real value for me you won't desire it. Believe me, I shall ever have a sincere love and esteem for you, who are the same, or more to me, than ever.

Tell me your thoughts in a letter, and suddenly, for I'm impatient till I hear from you.

Pride and indignation seized me at the reading of this, in a style so different from the former. What his dependence upon his sister, in point of interest, was I could not tell. But I thought, be it never so great, he made too large a sacrifice to it and such as love could never forgive him. That I was discovered and my honour wrongfully suspected was not half my concern, though that must needs sensibly affect a soul haughty like mine and who would rather meet death than shame.

I would give him my answer next morning, wherein I complained of the weakness of that love which could not stand one assault. The rest you may conclude by his reply.

THE THIRD LETTER
(in vindication of his doubted love)

What have I wrote that you interpret so much to my disadvantage? I am surprised at your answer. You take my meaning quite contrary to my intentions. Don't believe I can renounce and forsake you, in whom I have first my chiefest happiness. I can't express the tenderness of my affections for you. Believe me you shall never find the fervency of my love turned into coolness, or my sincerity into flattery, nor my soul guilty of an ingratitude. If you have any love for me, don't perplex yourself, for that gives me great uneasiness, nor imagine I can have one unkind thought for you. I love you most dearly well indeed. Time will produce it and convince you of the truth of all I say, when opportunity permits me to show how much, how unalterably I am yours.

I should not have given you these letters at length but only to beg your judgement of my lover's sincerity. He was some time before this about departing from us, upon his own business, with stupid Mrs Abigail for his housekeeper. I conceive Mrs Wouldbe was of use to him (she governing her husband) in point of stock or partnership – that made him so cautious of disobliging her.

She closeted him the next day, employing three hours in railing at me with the most prodigious, absurd abuses that envy or malice or the devil himself could invent. Who does not know the power of an ill tongue upon weak minds? He ought to have considered it, that interest and revenge dictated to them, and have, with fortitude and justice, withstood any impression they would have made upon him. I believe indeed he was proof to a great part of it till, industriously, Mrs Marwould (owing me a good turn for preventing her a conquest she had a desire to) told him I was a lady only seeking my diversions and in whom vanity so much prevailed as to expose his letter to her and then repeated part of what she had cunningly read over my shoulder. He persisted in his denial that he had never writ to me any but, when we next met, I found his eyes declined me and no longer animated by those bewitching softening glances that sweetened all the cruelties of fortune and which love of me first taught. I pursued 'em but they were lost to me.

I found time to ask the cause of the change. He answered I had exposed his letter, 'twas that he could not account for and therefore must begin to practise a difficult care upon his heart, since I did but laugh at him. I had not leisure to answer but, upon paper, endeavoured to convince him how the matter happened. This gave me more pain than I can express. If they could succeed in such common arts of making a misunderstanding between us, 'twas in vain for me to expect the prospect of any happiness. I suffered more real anguish by his false displeasure than I can describe.

My letter wrought so far upon him that, at the next meeting, I found the kindling fire returning to his eyes and when, upon the first opportunity, he caught me in his arms to kiss me, I felt the same ease, the same release from pain as a wretch took from the rack, or from that more exquisite torture, the rack of nature, the ease a woman feels released from mother-pains.

He said he had in vain strove for his cure. The more he strove, the harder it was to conquer. But, my Clorinda, I found how dear I was like to pay for that letter which had so transported me. Oh, why must the extremity of pleasure produce the extremity of pain?

I found his mind daily shaken even from its foundation. He never would believe but that I had exposed his letter. And all that could be said was that he endeavoured to forgive it me. But 'twas a weakness he did not think I could have been guilty of. And if on the side of love I lost no ground with him, I suffered much and wrongfully in his esteem, besides the pain I had been in, taught him the power he had over me and which, upon all occasions, he too much exerted, perplexing me as he pleased, taking delight in the alternate pains and pleasure that he could raise in me and which I can't forgive him for.

This was all done by snatches, for, since the first discovery, I had never so much as one quarter of an hour's time to talk the matter over with him.

Thus stands the present state of our amour. He is gone to his own house, distant from ours. These three long, tedious days and nights I have lived, and lived without one sight of him.

Tell me sincerely, my Clorinda, thou infallible judge of hearts, what dost thou believe of him? Could I but find myself in earnest slighted, pride and disdain in my haughty soul must cure me, for though I so long, against my will, persisted, constant to my first engagements, it was because our separation was the work of cruel fortune, in which unkindness had not any part.

'Twill be vain to expect my cure from reason, for that points to mutual love as the greatest good. I am not, my Clorinda, born to happiness – when young, betrayed and married where I could never affect, you know the next, how my first dear inclinations were crossed. See if I have any better hopes of this. Fortune cruelly is against me. I can't hope not to be happy.

Oh, restore me then by your wise counsels to that blessed state of indifferency, extinguish in me, if it be possible, these eternal sparks of love, or teach me to transfer it to a brighter, a more worthy object. Improve this human to a wholly divine. Let me there only fix my eternal hopes of unfading joys, of pleasures

unknowing a decay, where, without reproach, it will be meritorious to excel in fondness, there only, where excess of passion gives,
without remorse, excess of pleasure, free from those allays attend-
ing transitory joys. Oh, aid me here to fix my hopes, my happiness, without end and without change, as I am yours.

FACTS

*It is impossible to back this chapter with facts because of the nature of the
story itself.*

10

Country Retreat

Mrs Manley spent the spring of 1704 in London, where she received a letter from her friend, the poetess Sarah Fyge, asking her to spend a few weeks with her in her Buckinghamshire home.

COURT INTRIGUES,
letter VIII, pages 48–9

Dear Madam,
I am pleased at your kind determination [*line missing from text*] for two months, and should be more so could I hope such a solitude would be any ways agreeable to you. Your welcome to me will be like a Prince to a peasant, where the sense of the honour is too much allayed by that of demerit.

I have neither Waller nor Dryden's *Fables*, therefore they'd be welcome. But pardon me that I dare ask anything with you, who are yourself more than all, from the great Marot down to Garth.* I hope you'll honour our country with some of your gayer ornaments, since we shall quickly have, near my Lord W—'s, some horse races that will be adorned with some thousands of mounted beaus and coaches, and 'tis in your power to make the Beau Monde there. If you should not want room in the chariot I may perhaps be so happy to meet you.

Pray by way of preparation think what a dull solitude you are approaching to, to wander in unfrequented paths, no music but

---

*Clement Marot, the great poet of sixteenth-century France, and Samuel Garth, a physician, who published in 1699 a mock-heroic poem, 'The Dispensary', which was a great popular success, and known as the nine-day-wonder.

silly birds, no Park, no Beau, but a sacred cynic, no wit beyond a Cambridge pun, old gardens and orchards instead of a Spring Garden and an ancient mansion house in room of a gay ruel; nay, worse, must go to church once a week (or be obliged to search for an allowable excuse) and have grace said every day over an ill-dressed dinner too, perhaps.

But there is nothing shall not be made agreeable, as far as they are capable of amendment by, dear madam.

Yours, &c.

Whilst there she did attend the races at Quainton.

NEW ATALANTIS I
pages 154, 158–63

They were to cross a meadow where a numerous congress of coaches presented themselves, beauties resplendent, both by art and nature, cavaliers dressed en campagne and well-mounted, besides a swarm of populate of both sexes, a ridiculous medley of humankind, fantastically habited in fashions of all ages, and airs of none ... The occasion of that belle-assemblée was a chariot race. The prize consisted in two gold goblets and eight hundred crowns in gold.

She drew attention to:

the number of priests that swarm at all races and are the foremost in the diversions of the place, some mounted upon lean, lank horses, others starched up (them of the better sort) in little chariots, with an appropriated holy air, crammed with women and infants, gazing and betting and more earnest than any of the racers themselves.

Her hostess's husband, Thomas Egerton, was a priest, and Mrs Manley, already suspicious about the benefits of long-term romantic relationships, was an avid onlooker during the couple's frequent marital disagreements.

The sight was pleasant enough: an old, thin, raw-boned priest in his sacerdotal habit, combating his wife, who buffeted him again and seemed to be the aggressor. He had not only lost his hat and

peruke in the scuffle, but his face looked all over besmeared with
something, nobody could tell what, but at last it was known to be a
piping hot apple pie, out of the oven, which she had scalded him
with in a very handsome manner, but was so kind as to throw a
pound of butter immediately after to cool him again. His righteous
spirit, raised by the smart of the burning, catched hold of her top-
knot, to demolish that fabric. It was fastened so close to her head
that he pulled and pulled in vain. She shrieked out as he pulled,
and well she might, for he had tore a piece of her ear from her
head, which made the blood run down and was easier to come off
than the head-gear, which was so interwove with pins, top-knots,
false and true curls, that it stood impenetrable, like a rock buffeted by the waves . . .

As soon as they were parted, the priestess flounced out of the
house, called for her coachman and bid him put in his horses, for
away would she go (in that very condition) to sue for justice, if
there were any justice in the nation. The poor fellow durst not but
obey her, though he loved his master ten times better . . .

The good old gentleman had water brought him to wash off the
baked mask from his face.

The gazers dismissed from the gate, and then, after recovering a
little air, he begged . . . pity upon a poor man, who for his sins was
matched to a she-devil incarnate.

'You see what she is for a person, my good friends and new acquaintance,' said the priest. 'Nothing was ever so homely. Her
face is made in part like a blackamoor; flat-nosed, blubber-lipped.
There's no sign of life in her complexion. It favours all of mortality.
She looks as if she had been buried a twelve-month. Neither her
cheeks nor lips can claim any distinction, they all are of an earthy
hue. Her teeth rotten, or sweet, as the grave or charnel-house, and
yet the devil was in me – I married for love. Lord bless us! Love of
what? Not her good conditions I'm sure.

'But I am an old man, as you see, and she's a wit. That took me,
though I understood never a word of what she writes or says. Deliver me from a poetical wife and all honest men for my sake! She
rumbles in verses of atoms, Arctic and Antarctic, of gods and
strange things, foreign to all fashionable understanding. Because
she was ingenious I thought she'd have been a help-meet to my
memory, being something decayed. But she hates her duty to me
and to the gods and never goes to the temple above twice a year,

and then she falls into counterfeit fits. The bottle of hartshorn's* sent for and herself carried, in a languishing posture, home.

'Her tongue is at perpetual war. Her discourse one continued reproach, derogating from mine and my children's honour. If there be anybody present then she's sure to be most virulent. If I happen to bear it with heroic patience she is defeated and undone, falls into fits, beats herself to be revenged on me. She has often kicked all the bedclothes off and her own linen, till she has been stark naked, when the under-priest, the coachman and boy have all been holding of her down. Yet I've good reason to think all this but a sham, I mean her fits, for, if you'll let her alone, she'll come quickly to herself. But anybody that compassionates her, as people are apt to do, till they know her, she'll hold 'em tack from one frolic to another for four long hours, and then, to complete all, as if nothing had ailed her, she'll start up of a sudden and fall a-boxing of me courageously, or her chambermaid, or both.

'When she has had her revenge she's at ease, but if, by chance, she finds my mind unguarded against the bitter assaults of her tongue, and that I do fall into a passion, as it is not possible always for me to forbear, then she's pleased, then she's delighted, and finds her joy in my torments. Is this anything but the temper of a devil?

'The day before I'm to sacrifice she's sure to perplex me all night long on purpose to discompose and put my mind out of frame.

'I've often attempted, upon such occasions, to lie in another bed, but that won't do, I should be too much at my ease and that would be her hell. Up she comes, roaring, and stamps her foot impetuously and incessantly upon the door till 'tis broke open.

'She's as strong in her freaks as a grenadier. Then she falls a-howling and sobbing, tells me she can't sleep without me, and either forces me to rise to her bed, or comes to bed to me and is sure to keep me awake all night long with her scolding, as that's all her end and design. There's no intervals, no truce to be had with her.

'She has frighted away all my children, won't suffer one of them in the house; had once liked to choked my daughter, that's a woman grown, by flying upon her with her two hands about her throat. She had stopped her wind-pipe till the poor girl's tongue hung out of her mouth and her face was grown black and had cer-

*Hartshorn: smelling salts.

tainly killed her in a few minutes more if I had not come in and prevented her.

'What safety, think you, can my life be in with such a fury? And
yet I know not what's the remedy. She won't go from me if I were
to give her all I have, though she's sordidly covetous, because she
dares not torment anybody else as she does me. And yet I keep her
a coach and four servants, have plentiful income and an estate of
my own, and she had little or no fortune.

'I was bewitched to marry her.

'Then she's in love with all the handsome fellows she sees. But
her face, I believe, protects her chastity, for none sure was ever yet
so courageous to assault it.

'She vents her passion in love verses and dialogues of Clarinda
and Daphnis. A pitiful lawyer's clerk was a long time her Alexis,
and there was love letters and verses printed with rattling epithets, bombast descriptions, romantic flights and, in short, nothing of nature in 'em, yet these must be printed, with an epistle
to her adored Moneses, who I've understood since was a foolish
apothecary, that used to recover her from her fits without the
help of Galen or Hippocrates.

'Then, for her morals, a lady whom she had invited to stay at our
house that summer [*Mrs Manley*], assumed the reasonable freedom to advise her against passion and anger, she took it so ill at
her hands that, to be revenged, she made herself a voluntary evidence in a law-suit against her, of all the discourse they had had
together in freedom, and by adding a great deal of false to the true,
made her lose her cause.'

THE FACTS

*It is more surprising to know that the two women had been friends than to
discover that they had fallen out.*

Sarah Fyge was born in London in 1669. In 1686 she published The
Female Advocate, *a reply to a satire by the scurrilous Robert Gould.*

*Her first husband, an attorney, was her 'Amintor'; her second, the raw-
boned priest, Thomas Egerton, was her 'Strephon'.*

*She was at least one of the Female Muses who wrote elegies upon
the death of Dryden in 1700. Three years later her* Poems on Several

Occasions, *together with* A Pastoral *were printed (appropriately enough) by J. Nutt.*

The poems bear witness to the rattling epithets and bombast descriptions.

A satyr against the muses[1]

By my abandoned Muse I'm not inspired,
Provoked by malice and with rage I'm fired.
Fly, fly, my muse from my distracted breast,
Whoe'er has thee must be with plagues possessed.
Fool that I was e'er to solicit you,
Who make not only poor, but wretched too.
Happy I lived for almost eight years time,
Cursed be your skill, you taught me then to rhyme.
The jingling noise shed its dark influence
On my then pleased, unwary innocence,
I scarce have had one happy moment since.
Here all the spite and rage of womankind
Cannot enough advance my threatening mind
Let furies too, be in the consort joined.
Passion, that common rage I here refuse,
Call Hell itself to curse my torturing muse;
Not the calm author of blest poetry
But the black succubus of misery.
There let her sit, with her infernal chime
And put the shrieks and groans of friends in rhyme.
. . .
Nothing like that to dangers can expose
May none be happy, but what write in prose.
Curse on the whimsical romantic fool
That yielded first to his fantastic rule:
That wit, like morris-dancers must advance
With bells at feet and in nice measures dance.
Let pregnant heads but think of poetry,
And just before the brain delivery
Fancy shall make a prodigy of wit,
Which soon as born shall run upon its feet.
Sure 'tis some necromantic ordinance
That sense beyond the circle mayn't advance.

Was all the learned ancients' courage dead
That wit, in fetters, is tame captive led?
Had some opposed when rhyme at first grew bold
Then her defeat not triumphs had been told?
But now the plague is grown so populous
'Tis hard to stop the universal curse.
Doubtless, they are mistaken who have told
Spiteful Pandora's pregnant box did hold
Plurality of plague, she only hurled
Out verse alone, and that has damned the world.
Curses in vain on poets I bestow;
I'm sure the greatest is that they are so;
Fate, send worse if thou canst, but rescue me
From trifling torturing wretched poetry.

One can only wish that her muse had found her and throttled her.

The law-suit was a premature attempt at palimony. Mrs Manley assisted Mrs Mary Thompson to get money from the estate of Mr Pheasant of Upwood, Huntingdonshire.

Mrs Thompson had lived with, and been kept by, Mr Pheasant, but when he died their relationship was not deemed sufficient to qualify her for kinship. Mrs Manley, with the help of Edmund Smith, a forger, resident of Fleet prison (presumably someone she had met through Tilly), attempted to establish right of dower out of Pheasant's £1500 p.a. estate on Mrs Thompson's behalf. Mrs Manley was to receive £100 p.a. in return for her services.

Smith swore that he had procured the priest, Dr Cleaver, parson of the Fleet, who had married Pheasant to Thompson, and that his friend Mr Abson had been present at the ceremony. Both Cleaver and Abson were conveniently dead. Smith was accused of making a false entry in the register at a church in Aldersgate Street, and this, with the weakness of their collateral evidence (and, perhaps, Sarah Fyge Egerton's evidence against them) led to the case being thrown out.[2]

Reassured of the advantages of her emotional independence, Mrs Manley returned to a literary career. This time, instead of the theatre, where success depends up on the cooperation of so many people, she turned her hand to a type of political writing very popular in France, the roman à clef.

Her Secret History of Queen Zara and the Zarazians (1705),

which exposed the less clean linen of the Churchills – John, Duke of Marlborough, and his wife Sarah – was a great success.

The following year, Almyna, a play derived from 'The Arabian Nights'
was performed by the Queen's Theatre Company with, again, Barry,
Bracegirdle and Betterton in the leads.

A collection of her correspondence, The Lady's Paquet Broke Open
was published in 1707, the year in which she took commissions for funeral
elegies for Edward and Cary Coke.

In May 1709 she brought out Secret Memoirs . . . from the New
Atalantis, Volume 1. A 246-page volume of contemporary gossip and
scandalous stories, it was an immediate success, and was read not only in
literary circles but by practically everybody who could read.

In July, in the person of Phoebe Crackenthorpe, 'a lady that knows
everything', she started work on the Female Tatler, a thrice-weekly news/
scandal sheet, and brought out the second edition of The New Atalantis
Volume I.

On 20 October, the eagerly awaited second volume of The New Atalantis was published.

Eleven days later, without any obvious build-up, Mrs Crackenthorpe resigned:

Mrs Crackenthorpe, resenting the affront offered to her by some
rude citizens, altogether unacquainted with her person, gives
notice that she has resigned her pretensions of writing the *Female
Tatler* to a society of Modest Ladies, who in their turns will oblige
the public with whatever they shall meet with that will be diverting, innocent or instructive.[3]

A few days later, at her country home, the writer and traveller, Lady Mary
Wortley Montagu, expecting delivery of a copy of The New Atalantis
Volume II, was getting restless:

Saturday came and no book. God forgive me I had certainly wished the
lady who was to send it me hanged, but for hopes it was to come by the
Nottingham carrier, and then I should have it on Monday, but after
waiting Monday and Tuesday I find it has not come.[4]

The book had been suppressed, and the publishers and printers taken into
custody.

1 Mrs S. F., *Poems on Several Occasions*, 1706, pp. 14–16
2 *Epistolary Correspondence of Sir Richard Steele*, ed. Nichols, II, p. 456

3 *The Female Tatler*, No. 51, Monday 31 October–Wednesday 3 November 1709 printed by A. Baldwin

4 *Letters of Lady Mary Wortley Montagu*, ed. Halsbad, I, p. 17

11

Grub Street

THE ADVENTURES OF RIVELLA
pages 108–17

Sir Charles Lovemore resumes:

I was in the country when the two first volumes of *Atalantis* were published and did not know who was the author, but came to town just as the Earl of Sunderland had granted a warrant against the printer and publisher.

I went as usual to wait upon Delarivier, whom I found in one of her heroic strains. She said she was glad I was come to advise her in a business of very great importance. She had as yet consulted with but one friend, whose counsel had not pleased her. No more would mine, I thought, but did not interrupt her. In conclusion she told me that herself was author of the *Atalantis*, for which three innocent persons were taken up and would be ruined with their families, that she was resolved to surrender herself into the messenger's hands who she heard had the Secretary of State's warrant against her, so to discharge those honest people from their imprisonment.

I stared upon her and thought her directly mad. I began by railing at her books, the barbarous design of exposing people that never had done her any injury. She answered me she was become misanthrope, a perfect Timon or man-hater, all the world was out of humour with her and she with all the world, more particularly a faction who were busy to enslave their sovereign and overturn the constitution, that she was proud of having more courage than had any of our sex and of throwing the first stone, which might give a hint for other persons of more capacity to examine the defects and vices of some men who took a delight to impose upon the world by the pretence of public good, whilst their true design was only to gratify and advance themselves.

As to exposing those who had never injured her, she said she did no more by others than others had done by her, i.e. tattle of frailties. The Town had never shown her any indulgence but, on the contrary, reported tenfold against her in matters of which she was wholly innocent, whereas she did take up old stories that all the world had long since reported, having ever been careful of glancing against such persons who were truly virtuous and who had not been very careless of their own actions.

Delarivier grew warm in her defence and obstinate in her design of surrendering herself a prisoner. I asked her how she would like going to Newgate. She answered me, very well since it was to discharge her conscience. I told her all this sounded great and was very heroic, but there was a vast difference between real and imaginary sufferings. She had chose to declare herself of a party most supine and forgetful of such who served them, that she would certainly be abandoned by them and left to perish and starve in prison.

The most severe critics upon Tory writings were Tories themselves who, never considering the design or honest intention of the author, would examine the performance only and that too with as much severity as they would an enemy's, and at the same time value themselves upon their being impartial, though against their friends. Then, as to gratitude or generosity, the Tories did not come up to the Whigs, who never suffered any man to want encouragement and rewards, if he were never so dull, vicious or insignificant, provided he declared himself to be for them, whereas the Tories had no general interest and consequently no particular, each person refusing to contribute towards the benefit of the whole and, when it should come to pass, as certainly it would, that she perished through want in a gaol, they would sooner condemn her folly than pity her sufferings, and cry, 'She may take it for her pains. Who bid her write? What good did she do? Could she not sit quiet as well as her neighbours and not meddle herself about what did not concern her?'

Delarivier was startled at these truths and asked me what then would I have her to do. I answered that I was still at her service as well as my fortune. I would wait upon her out of England and then find some means to get her safe into France, where the Queen that would have once been her mistress would doubtless take her into her own protection. She said the project was a vain one, that lady being the greatest bigot in nature to the Roman church, and she was, and ever would be, a Protestant, a name sufficient to destroy the great merit in that court.

I told her I would carry her into Switzerland or any country that was but a place of safety, and leave her there if she commanded me. She asked me in a hasty manner, as if she demanded pardon for hesitating upon the point, what would then become of the poor printer and those two other persons concerned, the publishers, who, with their families, all would be undone by her flight, that the misery I had threatened her with was a less evil than doing a dishonourable thing.

I asked her if she had promised those persons to be answerable for the event. She said no, she had only given them leave to say, if they were questioned, they had received the copy from her hand.

I used several arguments to satisfy her conscience that she was under no farther obligation, especially since the profit had been theirs. She answered it might be so, but she could not bear to live and reproach herself with the misery that might happen to those unfortunate people.

Finding her obstinate, I left her with an angry threat of never beholding her in that wretched state into which she was going to plunge herself.

Delarivier remained immovable in a point which she thought her duty, and accordingly surrendered herself and was examined in the secretary's office.

They used several arguments to make her discover who were the persons in the books, or at least from whom she had received information of some special facts which they thought were above her own intelligence.

Her defence was with much humility and sorrow for having offended, at the same time denying that any persons were concerned with her or that she had a farther design than writing for her own amusement and diversion in the country, without intending particular reflections or characters.

When this was not believed and the contrary urged very home to her by several circumstances and likenesses she said then it must be inspiration, because, knowing her own innocence, she could account for it no other way.

The secretary replied upon her that inspiration used to be upon a good account and her writings were stark naught. She told him, with an air full of patience, that might be true, but it was as true that there were evil angels as well as good, so, nevertheless, what she had wrote might still be by inspiration.

Not to detain you longer ... this poor lady was close shut up in the messenger's hands from seeing or speaking to any person, without being allowed pen, ink and paper, where she was most tyrannically and barbarously insulted by the fellow and his wife who had her in keeping, though doubtless without the knowledge of their superiors, for, when Delarivier was examined, they asked her if she was civilly used. She thought it below her to complain of such little people who, when they stretched authority a little too far, thought perhaps that they served the intention and resentments, though not the commands of their masters, and accordingly chose to be inhuman rather than just and civil.

Delarivier's counsel sued out her *habeas corpus* at the Queen's Bench Bar in Westminster Hall, and she was admitted to bail.

Whether the persons in power were ashamed to bring a woman to her trial for writing a few amorous trifles purely for her own amusement, or that our laws were defective, as most persons conceived, because she had served herself with romantic names and a feigned scene of action, but after several times exposing her in person to walk cross the court before the bench of judges with her three attendants, the printer and both publishers, the attorney general, at the end of three or four terms, dropped the prosecution, though not without a very great expense to the defendants, who were, however, glad to compound with their purses for their heinous offence and the notorious indiscretion of which they had been guilty.

There happened not long after a total change in the ministry, the persons whom Delarivier had disobliged being removed and consequently her fears dissipated. Upon which that native gaiety and good humour, so sparkling and conspicuous in her, returned. I had the hardest part to act, because I could not easily forgo her friendship and acquaintance, yet knew not very well how to pretend to the continuance of either, considering what I had said to her, upon our last separation, the night before her imprisonment.

Finding I did not return to wish her joy with the rest of her friends upon her enlargement, she did me the favour to write to me, assuring me that she very well distinguished that which a friend, out of the greatness of his friendship, did advise, and what a man of honour could be supposed to endure, by giving advice wherein his friend or himself must suffer, and that since I had so generously endeavoured her safety, at the expense of my own character, she would always look upon me as a person whom nothing could taint but my friendship for her. I was ashamed of the delicacy of her argument, by which, since I was proved guilty, though the motives were never so prevalent, still, my honour was found defective, how perfect soever my friendship might appear.

Delarivier had always the better of me at this argument and, when she would insult me, never failed to serve herself with that false one, success. In return, I brought her to be ashamed of her writings, saving that part by which she pretended to serve her country and the ancient constitution (there she is a perfect bigot from a long untainted descent of loyal ancestors, and consequently immovable). But when I would argue with her the folly of a woman's disobliging any one party, by a pen equally qualified to divert all, she agreed my reflection was just, and promised not to repeat her fault, provided the world would have the goodness to forget those she had already committed, and that henceforward her business should be to write of pleasure and entertainment only, wherein party should no longer mingle, but that the Whigs were so unforgiving they would not advance one step towards a coalition with any muse that had once been so indiscreet to declare against them.

She now agrees with me that politics is not the business of a woman, especially of one that can so well delight and entertain her readers with more gentle, pleasing themes, and has accordingly set herself again to write a tragedy for the stage.

THE FACTS

Narcissus Luttrell, in his Brief Relation of State Affairs, *confirms that on 29 October 1709, 'The publishers and printers of a late book called New atalantis, which characterizes several persons of quality are taken up, as also Mrs Manley, the supposed author.'*[1] *The publishers were John*

Morphew and J. Woodward; the printer, John Barber. At this stage Mrs Manley's own version is confirmed for she is understood only to be the 'supposed' author.

Four days later she has convinced them of her own part in the proceedings for Luttrell writes: 'Today the printer and publisher of the New atalantis were examined touching the author, Mrs Manley; they were discharged but she remains in custody.'[2]

She was admitted to bail on 7 November 1709.[3]

Her trial was heard on 11 February 1710, the last day of term, at the Queen's Bench Court. She was discharged.[4]

Her play Lucius, the First Christian King of Britain, was performed at Drury Lane Theatre in May 1717.[5]

1 Luttrell, p. 505
2 Luttrell, p. 506
3 Luttrell, p. 508
4 Luttrell, p. 546
5 Emmett L. Avery, *The London Stage 1700–1729*, p. 450

12

The Adventures of Rivella

Undaunted by her spell in captivity Mrs Manley went on to publish two volumes of Memoirs of Europe, *as sequels to* The New Atalantis, *and continued writing on her specialist subject, political scandal and social intrigue:* The Duke of M—h's Vindication, A Learned Comment on Doctor Hare's Sermon, A True Narrative of . . . the Examination of the Marquis de Guiscard, A True Relation . . . of the intended riot on Queen Elizabeth's Birthday *(1711) and* The Honour and Prerogative of the Queen's Majesty Defended *(1713). During this time she also worked with Jonathan Swift on the* Examiner *and took over editorship on his retirement in 1710. The* New Atalantis, *which had brought her into the hands of the law, was frequently reprinted.*

Her husband, John, died at one o'clock on the 16 December 1713.

It is difficult to see clearly how their relationship stood. She wrote as disdainfully of him after his death as before, but there are common points which indicate that they had maintained some contact.

John Manley did vote against the bill to prevent the release of debtors from prison (see Chapter Seven); he was on the committee to draw up an address on Guiscard's attempt on the life of Harley. Mrs Manley wrote an exposé of the Guiscard affair; he hinted to Parliament that John Churchill was not quite the patriot he seemed, and he and Mrs Delarivier Manley were said to have been in frequent communication with the Jacobite Court during the reign of Queen Anne.[1] It was suspected that John Manley had Jacobite connections and if the authorities also suspected that Dela still communicated with him it would explain why she was quizzed in her trial as to who had given her 'information of some special facts'. It appears that the judge was actually gunning for the source of apparent government leaks in the person of John Manley MP.

As he died intestate there is no documentary evidence of his latter relationship with Delarivier or their son.

Days later, at Christmas 1713, still heirless, Queen Anne fell dangerously ill. In Parliament the Whigs and those Tories who supported the Hanoverian succession acted in concert. The country was not confident enough in its future to enjoy criticism of its present.

Mrs Manley had one last burst of Tory patriotism in her Modest Enquiry (1714) and then, after Queen Anne's death, which brought with it Whig supremacy under George I, she seems to have retired from the political arena.

In the early spring of 1714, she was living with her sister Cornelia Markendale and John Barber (who had printed The New Atalantis, the Examiner and went on to print Lucius and The Power of Love) at the printing house on the corner of Old Fish Street and Lambeth Hill.[2]

John Barber was also an alderman of the City of London and went on to become Lord Mayor. Born in 1675, the son of a London barber, he was clothed, housed and packed off to school in Hampstead by the playwright Elkanah Settle, author of The Empress of Morocco and other heroic dramas. Settle then bound him apprentice to a printer's widow in Thames Street.

In 1700 he opened his own printing house in Queen's Head Alley, and afterwards moved to Lambeth Hill where 'his fame . . . drew the beaux and belles . . . tho' . . . neither could have anything to do with the printer tho' they might with the man.'[3]

In 1720 Barber made upwards of £30,000 in South Sea Stock, while everyone around him was ruined.

His death in 1741 brought a rush of pamphlets describing his 'true' character: 'His intimate friends he treats like his dependants, his dependants like his footmen and his footmen like his slaves.' There has been much speculation as to whether Barber's relationship with Mrs Manley was purely business or whether she was also his mistress. His biographer asserts that 'he was often inclined to marry, but the expense of a wife he could never reflect on without melancholy. And the most effectual way he took to cure himself of that expensive tendency to marriage was by calculating and computing how much such a companion might annually cost him.' To such a parsimonious householder Mrs Manley had one big advantage: she contributed handsomely to the household finances with the profit from her writings. She is said to have got him many thousands of pounds – not to mention the introductions she effected for him: Lord Bolingbroke, Robert

Harley, Jonathan Swift, Matthew Prior. This alone could explain the tone of her letters to the rival printer Edmund Curll.[4]

Curll, who became one of Pope's dunces in The Dunciad, *was not a man famed for high literary standards. Twice he was brought before the bar of the House of Lords for publishing material relating to members of the House, he was tried and convicted of printing obscene books, and fined for publication of* The Nun in her Smock *and* De Usu Flagorum. *Other books on his list include* The Boarding School Rape *and* The Altar of Love; or the whole Art of Kissing. *His fame for publishing monographs on the lives of the recently dead led the physician and wit Arbuthnot to say that he added a new terror to death. Curllicism became a synonym for literary indecency.*

Early in 1714 Mrs Manley heard that Charles Gildon, a prolific Grub Street hack, was starting work on 'a severe invective on some part of her conduct' under the title 'The Adventures of Rivella'. Edmund Curll brought the two writers together privately in his Fleet Street home. Surprisingly, Gildon stood down, and Mrs Manley agreed to write the book for Curll, keeping Gildon's title. On 15 March, she wrote:

I am to thank you for your very honourable treatment, which I shall never forget. In two or three days I hope to begin the work.

I like your design of continuing the name and title. I am resolved to have it out as soon as possible. I believe you will agree to print it as it is writ.

When you have a mind to see me, send me word and I will come to your house, for, if you come upon this Hill, B. will find it out. For god's sake let us try if this affair can be kept a secret.

I am, with all respects, sir, your most obliged, humble servant,

D. Manley

P.S. I have company, and time to tell you only that your services are such to me that can never be enough valued. My pen, my purse, my interest are all at your service. I shall never be easy till I am grateful.

A week later she wrote again:

Judge that I have not been idle when I have sent you so much copy. How can I deserve all this friendship from you?

I must ask you to pity me, for I am plagued to death for want of time and forced to write by stealth.

I beg the printer may not have any other to interfere with him, especially because I shall want time to finish it with the éclat I intend.

I dread the noise 'twill make when it comes out. It concerns us all to keep the secret... Though the world may like what I write of others, they despise whatever an author is thought to say of themselves.[5]

She enclosed the manuscript of Rivella. It was the last truly autobiographical piece she was to write.

She spent the summer of 1714 with her sister at the home of Mr Partridge in Whetstone, Finchley Common, plagued by threats of retribution from Marlborough's supporters and her own rather embarrassing situation: she had no mourning clothes and dared not appear in London without as Queen Anne had died.[6]

From 1714 till her death in 1724 she spent her winters at Lambeth Hill and her summers in Beckley, Oxfordshire, where she had a house. A neighbour, James Moore Esq., described the effect she had on the 'empire of a country village': 'The bright contagion, as our young friend calls it, of that lady's romance has spread itself through this whole place. Everything moves in that spirit. Horses are palfreys; sweethearts, paramours; and west-winds Etesian gales. The women all take their names from Grand Cyrus.'[7]

In 1717 Steele's company at Drury Lane presented her most successful play, Lucius. *It was revived in 1720, the year which also saw the publication of her last known work, a collection of seven novels taken from Painter's* Palace of Pleasure *entitled* The Power of Love.

Eventually, like all the men in her life, John Barber let her down. When he looked ill, she suggested a trip to Naples. He went alone, with £50,000 in bills of exchange for the Old Pretender. On his return journey he hesitated at Calais, afraid to cross the Channel because of the meetings he had had with the Jacobites, including the Chevalier de St George himself, who gave him a ring.

'Here opens a scene of the blackest ingratitude to his best friend, Mrs Manley, through whose interest all those persons who contributed to make his fortunes were owing, besides the large sums he acquired from her writings.' Instead of asking his 'polite mistress', Mrs Manley, to join him, he sent for 'one of his adorable modern spinsters', Sarah Dovekin, whom he had hired in the country and brought up to Town 'to attend Mrs Manley in the lowest degree of servitude', so that 'Lady Barber of Calais in brocade

wore the plain stuff-gown in England.' It was said that though he was a 'tyrant . . . he might be said to assume brute in forsaking the polite mistress to take up with the ignorant serving wench.'[8]

On 29 February, 1724, the Weekly Journal *reported her dangerously ill.*

Two days later, Curll wrote to Sir Robert Walpole asking for 'some provision in the Civil List' in exchange for the information that Mrs Manley had prepared a fifth volume of The New Atalantis, *which was printed and ready for publication.*[9] *According to the author of the* Impartial Life of Mr Barber, *she 'had made a considerable progress in a second volume of novels, but Barber's latter behaviour put a stop to her finishing it.'*[10]

She died at Barber's house on 11 July, and was buried in the church of St Benet's, Paul's Wharf, under a white marble stone inscribed

> *Here*
> *Lyeth the Body of*
> *Mrs DELARIVIER MANLEY*
> *Daughter of Sr Roger MANLEY Knight*
> *Who suitable to her Birth & Education*
> *was acquainted with several parts of knowledge*
> *And with the most polite writers*
> *Both in the FRENCH and English Tongue*
> *This Accomplishment together*
> *With a great natural stock of wit*
> *Made her conversation*
> *Agreeable to All who knew her*
> *And her writings*
> *To be universally read with pleasure*
> *She dyed July 11 Anno Dom 1724*

In her will she only mentions two plays by name and requests that 'All my other manuscripts whatever I desire may be destroyed, that none ghost-like may walk after my decease, nor any friends' letters to me, nor copies of mine to them, or, in a word, nor the least from my papers be published but the said tra. and com.'[11]

Either a relative or an over-zealous representative of the government carried out their orders too thoroughly. Any other works by Mrs Manley, including the two plays, are lost or destroyed.

In Somerset House gardens Sir Charles Lovemore's tale of an extraordinary woman is coming to an end.

1 HMC Downshire, vol. 1, p. 883
2 Cornelia Manley's licence to marry John Markendale was issued 10 May 1698. (G. Cokayne and E. Alexander Fry, Calendar of Marriage Licences granted in the Faculty Office, 1905, p. 150) presumably he had died or they had separated by this time; evidence that she lodged at Barber's is in her letters – Harley Papers, 29/203, pp. 453, 458
3 *Impartial History of the Life, Character, Amours, Travels and Transactions of Mr John Barber*, by several hands (printer T. Cooper), 1741, pp. 2–9
4 *Impartial History of . . . Mr John Barber*, pp. 8, 40
5 Both letters quoted in Curll's introduction to the 1725 edition of *Rivella*, entitled *Mrs Manley's History of her own Life and Times*, pp. iv–vi
6 Harley Papers 29/204, p. 491
7 *Mr Pope's Literary Correspondence*, III, 1735–7, p. 9
8 *Impartial History of . . . Mr John Barber*, pp. 24, 44
9 Curll, ibid, p. vii
10 *Impartial History . . . of Mr John Barber*, Civis, p. 47
11 Her will, proved 28 September 1724, PROB 11/599/194–5

Epilogue

THE ADVENTURES OF RIVELLA
pages 117–20

'But has she still a taste for love?' interrupted young Monsieur D'Aumont.

'Doubtless,' answered Sir Charles, 'or whence is it that she daily writes of him with such fire and force? But whether she does love is a question. I often hear her express a jealousy of appearing fond at her time of day and full of raillery against those ladies who sue when they are no longer sued unto. She converses now with our sex in a manner that is very delicate, sensible and agreeable, which is to say, knowing herself to be no longer young, she does not seem to expect the praise and flattery that attend the youthful. The greatest geniuses of the age give her daily proofs of their esteem and friendship, only one excepted [Steele again], who yet I find was more in her favour than any one of the wits pretend to have been, 'twas his own fault he was not happy, for which omission he has publicly and gravely asked her pardon. Whether this proceeding was so, Chevalier, as it ought I will no more determine against him, than believe him against her, but since the charitable custom of the world gives the lie to that person, whosoever he be, that boasts of having received a lady's favour, because it is an action unworthy of credit and of a man of honour, may not he by the same rule be disbelieved, who says he might, and would not, receive favours, especially from a sweet, clean, witty, friendly, serviceable and young woman, as Rivella was, when this gentleman pretends to have been cruel, considering that he has given no such proof of his delicacy, or the niceness of his taste.

'But, what shall we say, the prejudice of party runs so high in England that the best natured persons, and those of the greatest integrity, scruple not to say false and malicious things of those who differ from them in principles, in any case but love. Scandal between Whig and Tory goes for nothing. But who is there besides myself that thinks it an impossible thing a Tory lady should prove frail, especially when a person (though never so much a Whig) reports her to be so, upon his own knowledge.

'Thus, generous D'Aumont, I have endeavoured to obey your commands in giving you that part of Rivella's history which has made the most noise against her. I confess, had I shown only the bright part of her adventures I might have entertained you much more agreeably, but that requires much longer time, together with the songs, letters and adorations innumerable from those who never could be happy.

'Then, to have raised your passions in her favour, I should have brought you to her table, well-furnished and well-served, have shown you her sparkling wit and easy gaiety when at meat with persons of conversation and humour, from thence carried you (in the heat of summer after dinner) within the nymph's alcove, to a bed nicely sheeted and strowed with roses, jessamines or orange-flowers, suited to the variety of the season, her pillows neatly trimmed with lace or muslin, stuck round with jonquils, or other natural garden sweets (for she uses no perfumes) and there have given you leave to fancy yourself the happy man with whom she chose to repose herself during the heat of the day, in a state of sweetness and tranquillity.

'From thence conducted you towards the cool of the evening, either upon the water, or to the park for air, with a conversation always new, and which never cloys.'

'Allons, let us go, my dear Lovemore,' interrupted young D'Aumont, 'let us not lose a moment before we are acquainted with the only person of her sex that knows how to live and of whom we may say, in relation to love, since she has so peculiar a genius for, and has made such noble discoveries in that passion, that it would have been a fault in her not to have been faulty.'

Postscript

In her will Mrs Manley asked to be buried under a white marble stone in the churchyard nearest to her London home. She also requested that her 'grave may be fenced in with iron rails to preserve it from being disturbed'.

Her executors took her wishes even further and she was buried inside the church. Unfortunately, the number of burials in the Wren-designed church during the following two centuries seriously undermined the foundations of the building and led to parts of the floor ominously rising. As a result the entire floor had to be excavated and layers of bones were skimmed off and (in some confusion) reburied elsewhere.

It is ironic that even after death Mrs Manley's best-laid plans should have failed so dramatically.

Chronology

LIFE	WORK
1688 Death of Sir Francis	
1689 Care of John Manley	
1691 24 June, birth of son	
1693 Death of brother Francis	
1694 Care of Lady Castlemaine	
Journey to Exeter and	
beyond	
1695 Back in London	Poem on *Agnes de Castro*
1696 Friendship with Skipwith	Letters written by Mrs Manley;
	The Lost Lover; The Royal Mischief
1697–1701 Affair with John Tilly	
1702 Tilly in debt	
Summer with Sarah Fyge	
Tilly marries	
1703 Probable trip to Bristol	
1705	*The Secret History of Queen Zara and the Zarazians*
1707	*Almyna; The Lady's Paquet Broke Open*
1709 Arrested	The *Female Tatler; The New Atalantis* (2 vols)
1710 Case dismissed	The *Examiner; Memoirs of Europe* (2 vols)
1711	*Court Intrigues; The Duke of M—h's Vindication; A Learned Comment on Dr Hare's Sermon: A True Narrative of . . . the Examination of the Marquis De Guiscard; A True Relation . . . of the Intended riot and tumult on Queen Elizabeth's Birthday*
1713 Death of John Manley	*The Honour and Prerogative of the Queen's Majesty Vindicated and Defended*
1714 Death of Queen Anne	*The Adventures of Rivella;*
Summer in Finchley	*A Modest Enquiry*
1715? Acquires house in Beckley	
for summers	

LIFE		WORK
1717		*Lucius, The first Christian King of Britain*
1720		*The Power of Love* (seven novels)
1724	11 July she died	
1725		*Bath Intrigues; A Stagecoach Journey to Exeter*

Key to Pseudonyms

ACTUAL	FICTIONAL
Lord Bath	Lord Meanwell
James Carlisle	Lysander
Lady Castlemaine	Hilaria
Charles II of Spain	Charles III
John Churchill	Count Fortunatus
Cornelia	Cordelia
Delarivier	Rivella
Lord Chancellor	Grand President
John Manley	Don Marcus
John Manley	Oswald
Mary	Maria
Monmouth	Count de Grand Monde
Lord Montagu	Lord Crafty
Mrs Pym	Mrs Settee
Sir Thomas Skipwith	Sir Peter Vainlove
Richard Steele	Monsieur L' Ingrat
Lord Sunderland	Lord S—d
John Tilly	Cleander
Catherine Trotter	Calista
William III	Henriquez

IN PROLOGUE AND EPILOGUE:

ACTUAL	FICTIONAL
Himself, a relation of the French Ambassador to London in 1714	Chevalier D'Aumont
John Tidcomb	Sir Charles Lovemore
Delarivier Manley	Rivella

PLACE NAMES:

ACTUAL	FICTIONAL
London	Angela
Hyde Park	The Prado

The Complete Works of Delarivier Manley

The Adventures of Rivella, or The History of the author of Atalantis, with secret memoirs and characters of several considerable persons, her contemporaries, reissued as *Memoirs of the Life of Mrs Manley*. 1714, 1717, 1725.

Almyna, or The Arabian Vow. 1707

Bath Intrigues, In Four Letters to a Friend in London. 1725.

Court Intrigues in a Collection of Original Letters from the Island of the New Atalantis &c. 1711. Previously published as *The Lady's Paquet of Letters taken from her by a French privateer in her passage to Holland, or, The Lady's Paquet Broke Open*, which was appended to Madam D'Aulnoy's *Memoirs of the Court of England*. 1707, 1708 England. 1707, 1708

The Duke of M—h's Vindication, in Answer to a Pamphlet Lately Published Called Bouchain. 1711

The Examiner, co-writer 1710, editor and writer of Nos. 45–50.

The Female Tatler, by Mrs Crackenthorpe, a Lady That Knows Everything. 1709

The Honour and Prerogative of the Queen's Majesty Vindicated and Defended Against the Unexampled Insolences of the Author of the Guardian, in a Letter from a Country Whig to Mr Steele. 1713

A Learned Comment on Dr Hare's Sermon. 1711

Letters Written By Mrs Manley, reissued as *A Stagecoach Journey to Exeter, describing the humours on the road, with the characters and adventures of the company. In eight letters to a friend*. 1696, 1725 1696, 1725

The Lost Lover, or The Jealous Husband. 1696

Lucius, The First Christian King of Britain. 1717, 1720

Memoirs of Europe Towards the Close of the Eighth Century, Written by

Eginardus, Secretary and Favourite to Charlemagne, and Done into English by the Translator of The New Atalantis. 1710

A Modest Enquiry into the Reasons of the Joy Expressed by a Certain Sett of People upon the Spreading of a Report of Her Majesty's Death. 1714

The Power of Love in Seven Novels: The Fair Hypocrite, The Physician's Stratagem, The Wife's Resentment, The Husband's Resentment, The Happy Fugitives, The Perjured Beauty. 1720, 1741

The Royal Mischief. 1696

The Secret History of Queen Zara and the Zarazians, Wherein the Amours, Intrigues, and Gallantries of the Court of Albigion, During Her Reign, are Pleasantly Exposed; and as Surprising a Scene of Love and Politics Represented as Perhaps This, or any Other Age or Country, has Hitherto Produced. Supposed to be Translated from the Italian Copy, Now Lodged in the Vatican at Rome. 1705, 1707, 1709, 1711, 1712, and in French 1708, 1711

Secret Memoirs and Manners of Several Persons of Quality, of Both Sexes. From the New Atalantis, an Island in the Mediterranean, Written Originally in Italian. 1709, 1716, 1720, 1736 etc.

A True Narrative of What Passed at the Examination of The Marquis de Guiscard at the Cock-Pit the 8th of March 1710/11. His Stabbing Mr Harley and Other Precedent and Subsequent Facts Relating to the Life of the Said Guiscard. 1711

A True Relation of the Several Facts and Circumstances of the Intended Riot and Tumult on Queen Elizabeth's Birthday. Gathered from Authentick Accounts: and Published for the Information of All True Lovers of Our Constitution in Church and State. 1711

WORKS BY MRS MANLEY WHICH HAVE NEVER BEEN FOUND:

The New Atalantis (fifth volume)
The Duke of Somerset, a tragedy
The Double Mistress, a comedy

Select Bibliography

Anderson, Paul B., 'Mistress ... Manley's Biography', *Modern Philology*, vol. 33. 1936
    'Delariviere Manley's Prose Fiction', *Philological Quarterly*, 12
    Mary de la Riviere Manley: A Cavalier's daughter in Grub Street, diss. Harvard 1931
Carter, Herbert, 'Three Women Dramatists of the Restoration', *Bookman's Journal*, 13, 1925
Duff, Dolores, 'Materials towards a biography of Mary Delariviere Manley', diss. Indiana, 1965
Jerrold, W. C., *Five Queer Women*, 1929
Koster, Patricia *The Novels of Mary Delariviere Manley*, Gainesville, 1971
    'Delariviere Manley and the DNB', *Eighteenth Century Life*, 3, 1977
Needham G. B., 'Mrs Manley, an Eighteenth Century Wife of Bath', *Huntingdon Library Quarterly*, No. 3, April 1938
    'Mary De la Riviere Manley, Tory Defender', *Huntingdon Library Quarterly*, 12
Palomo, Dolores, *A woman writer and scholars*, Women and Literature, 1978
Sergeant, Philip W., *Rogues and Scoundrels*, 1924

Aitken G., *Life of Steele*, 1889
Anon, *The Impartial History of the Life, Character, Amours, Travels and Transactions of Mr John Barber*, 1741
    Life & Character of John Barber, 1741 (Printer: T. Cooper)
Betterton, Thomas (Gildon & Curll), *History of the English Stage*, 1741

Churchill, Winston S., *Marlborough, His Life and Times*, 1938

Cibber, Colley, *An Apology for the Life of Colley Cibber* (ed. Lowe), 1889

Clark, G. N., *The Later Stuarts*, 1961

Genest, John, *Some Account of the English Stage*, 1832

Hamilton, Elizabeth, *The Illustrious Lady*, 1980 (Castlemaine)

Hartmann, C. H., *The Vagabond Duchess*, 1926 (Mazarin)

Highfill, P. H., etc., *A Biographical Dictionary of Actors . . . 1660–1800*, 1973–

Hudson W. H., *Idle Hours in a Library*, 1897

Jacob, Giles, *The Poetical Register*, 1719

Kenyon, J. P., *The Stuarts*, 1966

Langbaine (Gildon), *The Lives and Characters of the English Dramatic Poets*, 1699

Leslie, J. H., *The History of Landguard Fort*, 1898

Luttrell, Narcissus, *A Brief Historical Relation of State Affairs*, 1857

Montagu, M. W., *Correspondence*, ed. Halsband, 1967

Morgan, Fidelis, *The Female Wits*, 1981

Needham, G. B. & Utter, R. P., *Pamela's Daughters*, 1937

Nichols, John (ed.), *The Epistolary Correspondence of Sir Richard Steele*, 1787

Nicoll, Allardyce, *A History of Restoration Drama: 1660–1700*, 4th ed., 1952

Oldmixon, John, *The Critical History of England* (1728–30)

Palmer, A. N., *A History of the Town of Wrexham*, 1893

Pepys, Samuel, *Diary*, ed. Latham, Matthews, 1970–76

Pope, Alexander, *The Rape of the Lock*, 1712
Mr Pope's Literary Correspondence, 1735–7

Straus, Ralph, *The Unspeakable Curll*, 1927

Swift, Jonathan, *Journal to Stella*, ed. Williams, 1948

Van Lennep, W. etc., *The London Stage*, 1966–

Wells, Staring B. (ed.) (Gildon), *A Comparison Between the Two Stages*, 1942

Wilson, J. H., *All the King's Ladies: Actresses of the Restoration*, 1958
Mister Goodman, the Player, 1964

Also see the following contemporary periodicals:

Examiner
Female Tatler
Guardian
Historical Register
Tatler
The Spectator
The Weekly Journal

Index